The Flying Boys in the Sky

Volume 1

Edward S. Ellis

Originally published in 1911

TABLE OF CONTENTS

5

Timely and fascinating stories of adventure in the air, accurate in detail and intensely interesting in narration.

CHAPTER I.
LEARNING TO FLY.

One mild summer morning in 1910, Ostrom Sperbeck, a professional aviator, stood on the edge of a broad meadow belonging to the merchant, Gabriel Hamilton, closely watching the actions of Harvey Hamilton, the seventeen-year-old son of his friend, to whom the lithe, smooth-faced German was giving his first lessons in flying an aeroplane.

It was on the return voyage from Naples to New York of the Italian steamer Duca degli Abruzzi, that Mr. Hamilton and his boy made the acquaintance of the genial foreigner, who was on his way to the United States to take part as a competitor in several of the advertised meets in different parts of the country. The acquaintance thus begun ripened into a strong friendship and the Professor became the guest of the merchant, who was a commuter between his country residence and the metropolis.

The youth, like thousands of American boys, was keenly interested in the art of flying in the air, and the Professor was glad to undertake to give him instruction. The two went by train to Garden City, Long Island, where the elder found his new Farman biplane awaiting his arrival. Harvey mounted to the aluminum seat in front of the gasoline tank and engine, while his conductor placed himself a little below him in front, where his limbs had free play. The machine was pointed to the southwest and Harvey enjoyed to the full his first ride above the earth. His attention was divided between the wonderful moving panorama below and studying every action of the expert, who was as much at home on his elevated perch as when seated in the smoking room of the Duca degli Abruzzi, chatting with his friends. He noted the movements of the feet which controlled the vertical rudder at the rear, and the lever beside which the Professor sat and elevated or depressed the horizontal rudder on the outrigger in front, thus directing the ascent and descent of the machine.

A thrilling surprise awaited Harvey when, after two stops on the way for renewing the gasoline and oil, they reached the merchant's home. Professor Sperbeck wished to make a preliminary tour through the country which he had now visited for the first time, and he left his order at Garden City for the construction of a new biplane. The one that had been finished was sold to Mr. Hamilton, who made a birthday present of it to his son, it being a question as to who was the more pleased, Harvey or his parent.

Omitting other preliminaries for the present, let us return to the smooth, sloping meadow where under the eye of the German expert, the young aviator was receiving his first instruction in the fascinating diversion.

"I know that you did not let an action of mine elude you," said the Professor, "and you feel that you understand pretty much all."

Standing by the biplane, the smiling Harvey nodded his head.

"I have a dim suspicion in that direction."

"You can never make yourself an aviator without self-confidence, but you may have too much of it. In that case you become reckless and bad results are certain to follow. Nor can you learn by simply observing the conduct of another. You have a motto in your country about experience."

"It is Benjamin Franklin's,—'Experience keeps a dear school but fools will learn in no other,'" said Harvey, atremble with eagerness.

"Quite true; well, if you please, you may seat yourself."

The lad stepped forward and sat down, his feet resting on the cross lever below, while he grasped the upright control lever on his right.

"Suppose you wish to leave the ground and mount into the air?"

"I pull this lever back; the motion turns up the horizontal rudder out there in front and the auxiliary elevating rudder in the rear; when I have gone as high as I wish, I hold the rudder level, and when I wish to descend, I dip it downward."

"Nothing could be more simple; and when you desire to change your direction to the right or left?"

"I work this lever with my feet, as we do in tobogganing."

"You have two smaller levers on the left."

"They control the spark and throttle."

"We won't enter further into the construction of the machine at present. I am sure you were born to be a successful aviator."

The quiet assurance of these words vastly strengthened the confidence of Harvey Hamilton. He knew the Professor believed what he said, and who could be more capable of correct judgment? Then, as if fearing he had infused too much courage into the youth, the instructor added:

"So far everything seems easy and simple. We were fortunate on our way here, in having the most favorable weather conditions, but you are sure sooner or later to run into complex conditions. Columns of cold air are forever pressing downward and warm ones pushing upward. This constant conflict creates air holes and all sorts of twists and gyrations that play the mischief with aviators, unless they know all about them.

"You have seated yourself, but don't try to start till I give the word. I wish first to put you through a little drill. I shall call certain conditions and you must do the right thing on the instant. Are you ready?"

"Fire away," replied Harvey, on edge in his expectancy.

"Ascend!"

Like a flash the youth pulled the control lever back.

"Too far; lessen the angle."

He promptly obeyed.

"Volplane!"

Harvey pushed the lever forward, but not too far.

"Quite well; go to the right."

The youth started to shift the rear rudder with his feet and smiled.

"That is hard work."

"Why?"

"Because of the gyroscopic action of the propeller; it is much better to turn to the left, though I suppose one can manage a long turn to the right."

"The Wright brothers have no trouble in swinging that way."

"Because they use two propellers, revolving in opposite directions, thus neutralizing that gyroscope business."

"You are tipping to the left!" shouted the Professor.

On the instant the aviator swung the control lever to the right.

"You are caught in a fierce tempest."

Since Harvey could not well make the right evolution he replied:

"I should dive into it."

"That's right; never run away from a maelstrom. I suppose you feel competent to make a voyage through the air?"

"I don't see why I cannot," replied Harvey; "I studied everything you did on our way from Garden City and I think I know what to do in any emergency."

"Admitting that that is possible—which it isn't—it is all-important that before you leave the earth you should get acquainted with your machine."

"Ask me about its parts and see whether I am not."

"That isn't what I mean; you got that information from the answers to my inquiries at the factory at Garden City, which I asked for your benefit. You must be as familiar with the aeroplane as with your pony which you have ridden for years and feel as much at home in your seat as if you had occupied it for months. It will take time to acquire that knowledge."

"I am at home now," replied Harvey, who could not help thinking his friend was over-cautious.

"Your danger is of having too much self-confidence. Remember and do exactly what I tell you to do and nothing else."

The pupil assured his instructor of the strictest obedience.

"Very well."

The Professor stepped to the rear, grasped a blade of the propeller and gave it a vigorous swing. That set the motor going with its deafening racket, but it was so throttled that the machine stood still for a minute or two, Sperbeck holding back all he could with one hand until the pressure became too great to resist. Then the aeroplane began moving forward, with fast increasing speed. When it had traveled a hundred yards, Harvey grasped the lever ready to point the front rudder upward upon receiving the order from the Professor. The noise of the motor would have drowned the loudest voice, and the youth kept glancing around for the expected signal. But it was not made. Instead, the Professor motioned with one hand for him to circle to the left. Harvey was disappointed but did not hesitate for an instant. He came lumbering and lurching over the sward, and, shutting off the motor, halted a few paces in front of his instructor, who had lighted a cigarette.

"It is best to cut grass for two or three days," explained the teacher.

"It surely will not take that long," replied Harvey in dismay.

"I trust not, but no ascent will be attempted to-day."

Harvey forced himself to smile, though he made a comical grimace.

"Put me through the paces; I'm bound to learn this business or break a trace."

Several spectators had gathered on the edge of the field and were watching the actions of the two with the aeroplane. They would have come nearer had not Harvey warned them by a gesture not to do so. He did not mind their enjoying the sight, for they could do that when a little way off as well as if closer, but they were likely to get in his way, and hinder matters.

Again and again the biplane went awkwardly forward on its three small wheels with their rubber tires. The field contained ten or twelve acres, thus giving plenty of space for maneuvering. Once he came within a hair of running into the fence, because as it seemed to him the machine did not respond with its usual promptness, but he showed rapid improvement and the Professor complimented him on his success.

"I'm playing the part of a navigator of a prairie schooner," said the youth, "though they are drawn by animals instead of being propelled by wind. I suppose, Professor, that before the summer is over you will let me try my wings?"

"That depends upon how well you get on with your first lessons."

CHAPTER II.
BOHUNKUS JOHNSON.

Suddenly a shout came from the edge of the field, and a negro lad vaulted over the fence and ran toward the couple. As he drew near he called:

"Why didn't yo' tole me 'bout dis, Harv?"

"I did call at your house for you, but Mr. Hartley said you were asleep."

"What ob dat? Why didn't yo' frow a brick fru de winder and woke me up? Gee! What hab yo' been trying to do, Harv?"

The newcomer was about the same age as Harvey Hamilton, but taller, broader and larger every way. He was the "bound boy" of a neighbor and had been a playmate of the white youth from early childhood. He was as much interested in aviation as Harvey, and had been trying to build an air machine for himself, or rather helping his friend to construct one, but their failure was so discouraging that they gave it up. What was the sense of attempting such a task when Mr. Hamilton stepped in and bought one of the best of aeroplanes for his son?

Professor Sperbeck had met Bohunkus Johnson, being first attracted by his odd name and then by the willingness and good nature of the colored youth. Bunk, as he was generally called by his acquaintances, was much disappointed because he had not been present earlier, but no one was to blame except himself. Shoving his hands in his pockets, he walked about the aeroplane, which he had admired upon its arrival, inspecting and trying to understand its workings.

"Hab yo' flowed?" he asked, abruptly halting and looking at Harvey who retained his seat.

"Not yet."

"Why doan' yo' do so? What's de use ob fooling round here?"

"Professor Sperbeck thinks I should learn more before leaving the ground. How would you like to try your hand?"

Bohunkus took off his cap and scratched his head.

"I guess I'll watch yo' frow flipflaps awhile."

Harvey turned to the Professor, who shook his head.

"You don't wish to smash the biplane so soon. You will have enough tumbles without his help. If you are ready you may try it again."

By this time Harvey had become somewhat accustomed to the sensitiveness of the machine. It required slighter movements of the lever than he had supposed and the response was sometimes quicker than he expected. He understood what his instructor meant by insisting that an aviator should become familiar with his machine.

Bohunkus was asked to hold the rear of the aeroplane until the revolving propeller acquired more velocity. The dusky youth buried his heels in the dirt and held the framework with might and main. The pull rapidly increased, while he put forth all his strength, which was considerable. The Professor gave no help, but trying to keep his face straight, watched things. Despite all he could do, Bunk was compelled to yield a few inches. He still resisted desperately, but while he could not add to his power, the uproarious motor fast did so. Suddenly it made a bound forward, and Bunk sprawled on his face, with his cap flying off. His hold had slipped and the machine shot forward with a speed far greater than any one of the three could have reached.

"Hang de ole thing!" exclaimed Bunk, climbing to his feet and brushing the dust from his clothes; "what's de use ob it yanking a feller like dat?"

The roaring motor was too near for either of his friends to understand his words, but it was easy to imagine their substance.

When Harvey had completed his circuit of the field, Bunk asked that he might try his hand. He certainly was not lacking in assurance, but the Professor would not consent.

"You might do well, but the chances are you would not. You will get your chance after a time. You may ride with Harvey if you wish."

With some hesitation, Bunk climbed into the seat behind his friend.

"Am yo' gwine to go up?" he asked.

"Not at present. Why do you wish to know?"

"So I can jump if yo' don't manage things right."

He grasped one of the supports on either side and braced himself. Naturally he was timid, but it did not seem to him there could be much danger so long as they remained on the ground. Half way round the field, his self-confidence returned, and his dark face was lighted with a broad grin as the machine came to a stop near where the Professor was waiting.

"Why can't yo' fly fru de air by staying on de ground?" was the next bright question of Bohunkus; "dat would be as nice as habin' Christmas come on de fourth ob July, so yo' could slide down hill barefoot."

"Suppose I relieve you for awhile," suggested the instructor. Harvey sprang to the ground and Mr. Sperbeck took his place, indicating, when Bohunkus started to leave his seat, that he should remain.

A few minutes later, the negro received the shock of his life. The Professor allowed the aeroplane to rush over the ground until its speed must have been forty miles an hour. Then he pulled back the lever and it instantly began mounting into the air. Bohunkus did not comprehend what was going on until he was fifty feet aloft and still ascending.

He threw his head to one side and stared at the ground, which appeared to be rushing away from him with dizzying swiftness. For an instant he meditated leaping overboard and catching the earth before it got beyond his reach. He partly rose to his feet, but the distance was too great. He called to the Professor:

"Stop! I doan' feel well; let me git down. What's de use ob such foolishness?"

But there was too much uproar for the aviator to hear, and had he caught the words he would have given no attention. Bohunkus in his affright glanced across the field to where Harvey Hamilton was standing with his gaze on the machine. Harvey waved his hand and the simple act did much to bring back the courage of the negro.

"I guess I can stand it as well as him," was his reflection; "so go ahead."

The course of Professor Sperbeck might well give the youth a calmness which he could not have felt in other circumstances. He skimmed several miles over the country, rising five or six hundred feet in the air, and attaining a velocity of fifty miles an hour. He had been pleased with the aeroplane on the ride from Garden City, and was still more pleased upon trying it out again. It seemed to have gained a steadiness and sureness which it lacked before.

As has been said, the real test of an aviator's skill is not in sailing through the air where all is tranquil, but in starting and in landing. Professor Sperbeck had left the ground without the least difficulty and he now came down with the grace and lightness of a bird.

In the afternoon Harvey Hamilton resumed his lessons, the instructor complimenting his proficiency.

"If the conditions are favorable to-morrow, we shall leave the ground with you at the helm," he assured his pupil, when they gave over the attempts for the day. At the side of the field nearest the house, Mr. Hamilton had had a hangar built into which the aeroplane was run and the door carefully locked. It was natural that the neighbors should show much curiosity in the contrivance, and there was no saying what mischief they might do. Bohunkus felt so much concern on this point that he came over to his friend's home after the evening meal and joined them on the porch, where Mr. Hamilton was also seated.

"I think," said Bunk, "that we hadn't oughter leave dat airyplane by itself."

"We haven't," replied Harvey; "the building is strong and the door locked."

"But some folks mought bust off de lock and run off wid it; some ob dem people am mighty jealous ob me and yo', Harv."

"They are all good friends of ours," remarked the merchant; "I'm sure nothing is to be feared from them."

"I hopes not, but I feels oneasy."

"What would you suggest?"

"Dat some one keeps watch all night."

"Suppose you do it?"

"I'll take my turn wid Harv."

"Very well; when the night is a little farther along, Bunk, you may go out there and stand guard till say about midnight; then come to the house and wake up Harvey, and he will take his turn at playing sentinel."

"That soots me," Bunk was quick to say, knowing it would be much easier to keep awake during the first half of the night. So, while the others chatted as the evening wore on, the colored youth rose, yawned, stretched his arms and announced that he would go to his home not far off, tell Mr. Hartley and his wife of the arrangement and then assume his duties at the hangar.

Although he saw no call for all this extra care, Harvey was quite willing to divide the duty with his colored friend, but he meant that Bunk should come to the house and rouse him, for he could not be expected to stay awake. However, the young aviator dreamed so much of flying through the air, and was so absorbed with the entrancing scheme, that he was the first one to wake in his home. He sprang out of bed, as the sun was creeping up the horizon, and lost no time in hurrying out to the hangar to learn why Bohunkus had not called him, though he held a strong suspicion of the real reason.

As Harvey sped around the corner of the low, flat structure, the first object upon which his eyes rested was Bohunkus, stretched out on his back, his mouth open, and breathing loudly, as no doubt he had been doing through most of the night. Harvey left him lying where he was, and rejoined his folks with the story of what he had seen.

An hour later, Professor Sperbeck, accompanied by the merchant and Harvey, walked to the hangar to resume the instruction of the previous day. In the interval, Bohunkus had awakened and gone for his breakfast. He said nothing of his remissness and his friends did not refer to it, since they had more serious matters to hold their attention.

Mr. Hamilton was much pleased with the proficiency shown by his son, but did not stay long, since important business called him to the city. The day was a busy one for the young aviator, who was allowed to make a flight in the afternoon with the watchful Professor seated behind him. He had very few suggestions to make.

When Harvey came down to earth, he bumped rather energetically, but no harm was done, and on the third trial no criticism was made. Two more days were spent in practice and then the instructor said:

"You are prepared to make as long a voyage through the air as you wish, and without any assistance from me."

CHAPTER III.
THE AEROPLANE IN A RACE.

The barograph showed that the aeroplane was more than nine hundred feet above the earth and the anemometer, or small wind wheel, indicated that the speed was forty-odd miles an hour, with the propeller making a thousand revolutions a minute. It was capable of increasing that rate by twenty per cent. and the aviator was gradually forcing it to do so.

The youth who sat in front, with the long control lever in his right hand, was our friend Harvey Hamilton, who, under the instruction of Professor Ostrom Sperbeck, the German aviator, had become so expert that he felt equal to any emergency that was likely to occur during his aerial excursions. The small levers on his left, governed as we remember the spark and throttle, while the vertical rudders were operated by the feet. So long as the heavens remained calm or only moderate breezes were encountered, everything would go as smoothly as if he were treading firm ground, but there was no saying what troubles were likely to arise,—some of them with the suddenness of a bolt from the blue.

Harvey had his back to the tank, which held ten gallons of gasoline, or petrol as it is called on the other side of the ocean, and two gallons of oil, one being as indispensable as the other.

In the aluminum seat just in front of the tank was Harvey's passenger, the support being adjustable and capable of carrying two persons without threatening the center of gravity, provided care was used. This passenger has already been introduced to you under the name of Bohunkus Johnson, who was the bound boy of a neighboring farmer, Mr. Cecil Hartley. He was a favorite with his easy-going master, who sent him to the district school during winter and let him do about as he pleased at other times. He had picked up the simplest rudiments of a primary education and with the expenditure of a good deal of labor could write, though he scorned to pay any attention to so unimportant a matter as spelling.

Bunk and Harvey being of the same age, were playmates from earliest childhood. The fact that they were of different races had no effect upon their mutual regard. Being the son of a wealthy merchant, the white youth was able to do many favors for his dusky comrade, who, bigger and stronger, would have risked his life at any time for him.

Although this particular flight was made on a sultry summer afternoon, each lad wore thick clothing and a cap specially made for aviators, as a protection against wind and cold. The first intention of Harvey was to climb high enough in the sky to establish a record for himself that would make all other rivals green with envy.

But not yet. There was too much fascination in coddling to the earth, where the wonderful varied panorama was ever changing, and always of entrancing novelty and beauty.

Bohunkus having little to do except use his eyes enjoyed the visual feast to the full. At the beginning he studied the action of Harvey, seated at his feet, having in view that thrilling hour when he would be permitted to handle the levers and guide the airship through space himself.

"I can do it as well as him," he said to himself; "de machine sets on its three little wheels wid dere rubber tires, and de propeller am started so fast dat yo' can't see de paddles spin round; den dem dat am holding de same lets go and it runs 'bout fifty yards, like lightnin'; den Harvey pulls de big lever back and dat flat rudder out front am turned upward and de ting springs into de air like a scared bird and dere yo' am!"

As Bohunkus sat he grasped a bit of the framework on his right and a corresponding support on his left. This was not always necessary, for it was smooth sailing, but, as has been intimated, there was no saying when a sudden squall or invisible pocket or hole in the wind would shake things up, and force one to hold on for dear life. He leaned slightly forward and looked down at the world sweeping under him. They were skimming over a village, numbering barely a score of buildings, the only noticeable one being the white church with its tapering spire pointing toward the realm to which erring men were directed. Just beyond the dusty winding road disappeared into a wood a mile in extent, emerging on the other side and weaving through the open country until it could no longer be traced.

The river far to the left suggested a ribbon of silver, so small that several tiny sails creeping over it appeared to be standing still. To the right and front a large city was coming into clearer view. The spires, skyscrapers and tall buildings were a vast jumble in which he could identify nothing. He did not attempt even to guess the name of the place.

A railway train was just leaving the village below them on its way to the city in the distance. The youths saw the white puff of steam from the whistle, which signalled its starting, and the black belchings of smoke came faster and faster as the engine rapidly gained headway. Harvey slightly advanced the lever and the aeroplane began descending a little way in front of the train. The contestants in this novel race should be nearer each other to prevent any mistake and make the contest more exhilarating.

Two hundred feet from the ground, Harvey pulled back the lever and the flat rudder on the front outrigger became horizontal. The downward dip of the machine ceased and with a graceful curve glided forward on a level course. No professional could have executed the maneuver with more precision. Harvey during these few moments decreased the revolutions of the propeller so as not to draw away from the locomotive. The race should be a fair one, even if the result was not in doubt.

This lagging caused the biplane to fall somewhat to the rear and gave the train time to hit up its pace. The engineer and fireman had caught sight of the machine some minutes before, and eagerly accepted the challenge. Both were leaning out of the cab windows and the engineer waved his hand at the contestant aloft. The fireman swung his greasy cap and shouted something which of course the youths were unable to catch. The passengers had learned what was in the wind, and crowded the platforms and thrust their heads from the windows, all saluting the aviator and intensely interested in the struggle for mastery.

Harvey was too occupied with the machine to give much attention to anything else. He knew he could rely upon Bohunkus for all that was due in that line. The dusky youth was so wrought up that he came startlingly near unseating himself more than once. He leaned far over, circled his cap about his head and shouted and whooped and kicked out his feet with delight. The laughing passengers who stared into the sky, saw the black face with its dancing eyes, bisected by an enormous grin, which displayed the rows of perfect even teeth, and all learned what a perfectly happy African looks like.

Jim Halpine, the engineer, said grimly to his fireman:

"I've heard about their flying faster than anything can travel over the ground, but I'll teach that fellow a lesson. Old 39 can make a mile a minute as easy as rolling off a log; watch me walk away from him."

He "linked her up" by drawing the reversing lever back until it stood nearly on the center and dropped the catch in place. Then the puffs came faster and faster, and not so loud, and 39 rapidly rose to her best pace. Having done all he could in that direction, Jim kept his left hand on the throttle lever, and divided his attention between peering out at the track in front and glancing upward at the curious contrivance that was coursing through the air just above him. The fact that it was creeping up caused no misgiving, for that was manifestly due to the fact that he himself had not yet acquired full headway.

Harvey meant to get all the fun possible out of the race. He was certain he could beat the engine, but to do so "off the reel" would spoil the enjoyment. He would dally for a time and when defeat seemed impending, would dart ahead—always provided he should be able to do so.

The locomotive had a straight away run of seven or eight miles, when it would have to slow down for the city it was approaching. The race therefore must be decided within the next ten minutes.

Harvey Hamilton played his part well. The engine and train being directly under him, his view of them was perfect without detracting from the necessary attention to his biplane. He was just behind the last car when he knew from the appearance of things that the engineer had struck his highest pace. The youth speeded up the motor so as slightly to add to the propeller's revolutions, but he showed no gain in swiftness. He was only holding his place.

The shouting passengers shouted still more, if that could be possible, and called all sorts of tantalizing cries:

"Throw down your rope and we'll give you a tow." "Get out and run alongside of us!" "You ain't racing with a cow." "We're going some!"

Such and similar were the good-natured taunts, which produced no effect upon the aviators for they did not hear them. The most exasperating gesture was that of Jim Halpine the engineer, who leaned far out of his cab and gently beckoned to the youths to come forward and keep him company. The fireman stood between the cab and tender and imitated his chief.

Harvey Hamilton seemed to see and hear them not. Bending far over with the lever grasped, he acted as if trying to add to his speed by the pose, as a person in his situation will sometimes do unconsciously. His face was drawn, as if with tense anxiety, and there was not the shadow of a smile upon it. All the same he was chuckling inwardly.

Bohunkus Johnson was almost beside himself. At first he did not doubt that a crushing triumph would speedily come to him and his companion, but as the seconds flew by and there was no gain upon the train thundering over the rails, a pang of doubt crept over him.

"Go it, Harv! Put on more steam! What's de matter wid yo'?" he shouted, swinging his arms and hitching forward as if to add an impulse to their progress. "If yo' lose dis race I'll jump overboard and swim to land. Dem folks see me blushing now!"

Less than a minute later, the African shouted to unhearing ears:

"Glory be! Dat's de talk! Now we've got 'em!"

The aeroplane was overtaking the train. Though the gain was slow it was unmistakable.

CHAPTER IV.
TRYING FOR ALTITUDE.

Ah, but Harvey Hamilton was sly. He began slowly creeping up until his machine was directly over the rear passenger coach, there being three beside the express car. Had he dropped a stone from his perch, it would have fallen upon the roof of the last one. The exultant expression on the myriad of faces took on a tint of anxiety. The fireman yanked open the door of the fire-box and shoveled in coal. No need of that, for 39 was already blowing off, even when running at so high speed. Jim Halpine had drawn over the long reversing lever till it stood within a few inches of perpendicular and another shift would have choked the engine.

The young aviator held his place for a brief while and then began gradually drifting back again. Bohunkus Johnson groaned.

"Confound it! what's de use ob trying to be good?" he wailed; "dem folks will grin dere heads off. Harv! make tings hum!"

Heedless of him, Harvey was carrying out his own scheme. He saw that the game was his and he was playing with the locomotive. When gaining on it, the airship was not doing its best, and his slight retrogression was in order to make his victory more impressive. Each contestant was going fully sixty miles an hour. No. 39 could do no more, but the aeroplane had not yet extended herself. She now proceeded to do so, inasmuch as in the circumstances the struggle must soon terminate.

Having dropped well to the rear again, Harvey called upon the motor to do its best. Its humming took on the character of a musical tone, and the propeller spun around, twelve hundred revolutions to the minute. The keenest eye could detect nothing of the ends of the blades, and only faintly discern them nearer the shaft, as if they were so much mist.

And then the biplane forged bravely ahead. She moved steadily along over the roofs of the cars, one after the other, and pulled away from the engine whose ponderous drivers appeared to be spinning around with the dizzying swiftness of the propeller overhead. Jim Halpine was utilizing every ounce of power, but could do no more, for he was already doing his best. It humiliated him to be thus left behind, but there was no help for it.

In his chagrin he tried a little trick which deceived no one, not even the two victors. Pretending he detected something amiss on the rails, he emitted a couple of blasts from his whistle and shut off steam. It looked as if he was actuated by prudence, but the obstruction was imaginary.

Most of the passengers like true sportsmen cheered the winner. Even the grinning fireman circled his cap again about his tousled head, but the engineer was glum and acted as if the only thing in the world of interest to him was the rails stretching away in front. What did he care for airships bobbing overhead? They were only toys and could never amount to anything in the economy of life.

As for Bohunkus Johnson he could not contain himself. Harvey remained as calm as a veteran, and gave no attention to anything except his machine, but his companion stood up in the hurricane at the imminent risk of playing the mischief with the aeroplane's center of gravity, waved his cap and furiously beckoned the engineer not to lag behind. His thick lips could be seen contorting themselves and evidently he was saying something. Had the laughing passengers been able to catch his words—which they were not—they would have heard something like the following:

"Why doan' yo' trabel? Yo's only walking; we ain't half trying; can't yo' put on more steam and make us show what we can do? I'm plum disgusted wid yo'."

Harvey Hamilton did not speak. He was "letting out" the machine. He meant to learn what it could do. When several hundred yards ahead of the train, he lifted the lip of the rudder in front, and the structure glided upward until he was a quarter of a mile above the earth. Even then Bohunkus behaved so extravagantly that the aviator turned his head and motioned to him to cease.

"Can't doot, Harv! My mouf am so wide open dat it'll take me a good while to bring my jaws togeder agin, and I'm ready to tumble out head fust."

By and by the colored youth toned down enough to resume his seat and check his explosions of delight, though he looked around and waved his hand several times at the train which was now so far to the rear that his action was not understood.

"Gee! but it's getting cold!" he exclaimed some minutes later, with a shiver. He buttoned his thick coat to the chin, donned his mittens, and wondered what it all meant. He had never understood, though he had been told more than once, that temperature decreases with increasing altitude. He had objected to donning such thick garments when about to start on their flight, but Harvey was the boss and insisted.

Bohunkus's next surprise came when he looked between his feet. They were directly over the city noticed some time before, but the buildings were shrunken and mixed together in a way that even he understood.

The anemometer suspended at the side of Harvey Hamilton showed that the aeroplane was coursing through the air at the rate of not quite a mile a minute. With the low temperature caused by the altitude, the wind created in the still atmosphere cut the faces of the two like a knife, and even penetrated their thick clothing. Bohunkus turned up his coat collar, and drew his cap over his ears, but his feet ached. He hoped the aviator would soon strike milder weather, though the colored youth did not know whether it was to be sought for above or below.

"If it gits colder as yo' go up," he reflected between his chattering teeth, "it must be orful cold when yo' reach heben; I remember now dat I was tole something 'bout dat, but I thought dey was fooling me."

The front rudder still sloped upward, and Harvey showed no intention of dropping lower or even of maintaining the level already reached. He and his companion had started on a week or ten days' outing, and it struck him that now was as good a time as he was likely to have for making a notable record.

So the propeller kept humming and they continued to climb. A glance at the barograph by his side showed that he had reached five thousand feet; to this he added another thousand, then another, and he felt a thrill when the indicator made known he was close to nine thousand.

Although, as you may know, several aviators have mounted almost two miles, none had done so at the time of which I am now speaking. Harvey was near the limit, and he had but to persevere a little longer to achieve a grand triumph. But the cold was becoming almost unbearable. In the hope of moderating the piercing chill, he lessened his speed, but was not sensible of much improvement.

His unremitting attention was not needed and he turned his head and looked at Bohunkus. The sight made him laugh. The negro had not only drawn his upturned collar about his ears, with his cap sunk low over them, and his mittened hands shoved into his pockets, but he had shrunk within himself to that degree that only his staring eyes and the tip of his nose were visible. He was hunched together, and gave one of the best imitations imaginable of a young man freezing to death.

"I know his race doesn't like cold weather, but it won't hurt him," reflected Harvey with another look at his barograph. To his astonishment, he had made no perceptible gain during the last several minutes. He turned on full power and kept the forward rudder inclined upward. He waited awhile before examining the instrument again. So far as it could indicate he was not a foot higher than before.

He was mystified. What could it mean? With the propeller revolving more than a thousand times a minute, he ought to have risen a half mile higher.

"I never heard of anything like it; the explanation is beyond me."

With a thrill of misgiving, he glanced at the different parts of the machine. There were the two slightly curving wings, measuring thirty-five feet from tip to tip; the horizontal rudder on the front outrigger responded easily to the levers, as he proved by test; the ailerons or wing tips, one above the other, worked simultaneously and with the same ease; the ash which formed the foundation of the engine, the whitewood of the ribs, and the sprucewood of most of the structure, all scraped and highly varnished, did not show the least flaw. The rigidity which is indispensable in the framework was maintained throughout. The rubberized linen covering of the wings was taut and as smooth as silk, and the eye could not detect the slightest wire or thing out of gear.

"Professor Sperbeck never told me anything of this, though if he were here, he would understand it. I wonder whether we have climbed any farther."

Another inspection of the instrument failed to show that the biplane had ascended an inch.

"Can it be that our height has anything to do with it——"

Harvey Hamilton uttered an exclamation. The mystery was solved. The aeroplane had risen so high that the rarefied air refused to lift it farther. The propeller was whirling at its utmost velocity, but the cold, thin atmosphere could sustain no more. It was impossible, situated as he was, to go any higher.

"If Bohunkus wasn't with me, I could rise a half mile or more, but there's no use of trying it now. Some time I'll do it alone."

The limit marked was a trifle under nine thousand feet. It was a notable exploit, but, as we know, it has been surpassed by other aeroplanes, and more than doubled by aeronauts.

Another fact flashed upon Harvey: it was two hours since he and his companion had started on the flight that was destined to be a memorable one, and they were a hundred miles from home. There could be only a small amount of gasoline left in the tank, and it would be impossible to return without procuring more. Prudence urged that he should lose no time in doing so. He slowly advanced the control lever, the front rudder dipped downward and he began approaching the earth. Some minutes must pass before they should feel the pleasant change of temperature, but it could not be long delayed.

In the midst of his pleasant anticipations, Harvey was startled by a shriek from Bohunkus:

"We's gone, Harv!" he shouted; "nuffin can sabe us!"

CHAPTER V.
A WOODLAND EXPERT.

The aeroplane was caught in a furious snow squall. While descending it ran into the swirling tumult which in an instant enveloped it like a blanket, the myriads of particles filling the air so thickly that the terrified Bohunkus could not see the ailerons and even the aviator was partly shrouded from sight. Harvey Hamilton was faintly visible as he leaned over and manipulated the levers. Not only was the snow everywhere, but the machine itself was rocking like a ship laboring in a storm. It tipped so fearfully that the negro believed it was about to capsize and tumble them out. He shrieked in his terror, and held fast for life.

Harvey paid no heed to him. He had enough to engage his skill and wits. He recalled that Professor Sperbeck had told him what to do when caught in one of those elemental outbursts. Instead of running away from it, he headed for its center, so far as he could locate it, as the navigator does when gripped by the typhoon of the Indian Ocean.

Within five minutes of the aerial explosion, as it may be called, the biplane was sailing in the same calm as before. The sun was shining low in the sky and all was as serene as the mildest summer day that ever soothed earth and heavens. The gust had come and gone so quickly that it seemed like some frightful nightmare. The youths might have doubted the evidence of their senses, but for the reminder of the snowflakes on the wings, different parts of the machine and their clothing. They had entered so balmy a temperature, however, that the particles soon dissolved and left only a slight moisture behind them.

"Wal, if dat don't beat all creation," mused Bohunkus; "de fust ting I knowed I didn't know anyting and de next dat I knowed wasn't anyting. Wonder if Harv seed dat yell I let out when dat rumpus hit me on de side ob my head."

The aviator acted as if unaware of the dusky youth's presence. Knowing the gasoline was nearly gone, he centered his thoughts upon making a landing. To his astonishment he saw an immense forest below him, many miles in extent. This seemed remarkable in view of the fact that only a short time before he had sailed over a large city, which could not be far to the south. He would have turned about and made for it, knowing he could renew his supply of fuel there, and find accommodations for himself and companion. But the fluid was lower than he had supposed. It would not carry him thither and he must volplane, or glide to earth, the best he could.

It need not be said that a stretch of woods is the worst place in the world for an aeroplane to descend to the earth. In fact it is impossible to land without wrecking the apparatus and endangering the lives of those it is carrying.

The keen eyes of the youth were scanning the ground below when to his surprise he caught sight of a village of considerable size to the westward. Why he had not observed it before passed his comprehension. It was barely two miles distant and he was wondering whether he had enough gasoline left to carry him over the woods to the broken country beyond when he made a second and pleasing discovery. A short distance ahead an open space in the forest showed,—one of those natural breaks that are occasionally seen in wide stretches of wilderness. It was several acres in extent and seemed at that altitude to be free of stumps and covered with a sparse growth of dry grass, so level that it formed an ideal landing place. He did not hesitate to make use of it.

Now when an aeroplane comes down to earth, the greatest care is necessary to avoid descending too suddenly. A violent bump is likely to injure the small wheels beneath or the machine itself. The aviator therefore oscillates downward somewhat after the manner of a pendulum. When near the ground, he shifts his steering gear so that the machine glides sideways for a little way. Then he circles about or takes a zig-zag course, until it is safe to shut off power and alight. As our old friend Darius Green said, the danger is not so much in rising and sailing through the sky as it is in 'lighting.

Harvey Hamilton displayed fine skill, seesawing back and forth until at the right moment the three small wheels touched the ground, the machine under the slight momentum ran forward for two or three rods, and then came to a standstill. A perfect landing had been effected.

"Gee, but dat's what I call splendacious!" exclaimed Bohunkus; "it's jest de way I'd done it myself."

The aviator leaped lightly from his seat, and his companion did so more deliberately. He yawned and stretched his arms over his head. Harvey gave him no attention until he had examined the different parts of the machine and found them in order. Then he looked gravely at the African and asked:

"Didn't I hear you make some remark at the moment we dived into that snow squall?"

"P'raps yo' did, for de weather was so funny dat it war nat'ral dat I should indulge in some obserwation inasmuch as to de same."

"But why use so loud tones?"

"Dat was necessumsary on 'count ob de prewailing disturbance ob de atmospheric air wat was surrounding us."

"I'm glad to hear your explanation, but it sounded to me as if you were scared."

"Me scared! Yo' hurts my feelings, Harv; but I say, ain't yo' gwine to tie de machine fast?"

"What for?"

"To keep it from running away."

"It won't do that unless some one runs away with it; but, Bunk, we can't do any more flying till we get some gasoline and oil, and it doesn't look to me as if there is much chance of buying any in these parts."

"Mebbe we can git it ober dere."

"Where?"

"At dat house jest behind yo'."

Harvey turned about and met another surprise, for on the farther edge of the natural clearing stood a dilapidated log dwelling, with portions of several outbuildings visible around and beyond it.

"I must be going blind!" was his exclamation; "I came near passing this spot without seeing it and never noticed that house."

But the young man was hardly just to himself. In his concentration of attention upon a landing place, he had given heed to nothing else, and the descent engaged his utmost care until it was finished. It was different with his companion, who had more freedom of vision. Moreover, the primitive structure which the aviator now saw for the first time was so enclosed by trees that it was hardly noticeable from above.

No fence was visible, but a small, tumble-down porch was in front of the broad door, which was open and showed a short, dumpy woman, slovenly dressed and filling all of the space except that which was above her head, because of her short stature. Her husband, scrawny, stoop-shouldered, without coat, waistcoat or necktie, wearing a straw hat whose rim pointed straight upward at the back and almost straight downward in front, with a yellow tuft of whiskers on his receding chin, and a set of big projecting teeth, was slouching toward the two young men, as if impelled by a curiosity natural in the circumstances. The thumb of each hand was thrust behind a suspender button in front, and it was evident that he felt some distrust until Harvey Hamilton's genial "Good afternoon!" greeted him. His trousers were tucked in the tops of his thick boots, which now moved a little faster, but came to a stop several paces off, as if the owner was still timid.

"How'r you?" he asked with a nod, in response to Harvey's salutation; "what sort of thing might you be calling that? Is it an aeroplane?"

"That's its name; you have heard of them."

"I've read about them in the newspapers and studied pictures of the blamed things, but yours is the first one I ever laid eyes on."

Despite the uncouth manner of the man, it was evident that he possessed considerable intelligence. He stepped closer and made inquiries about the machine, its different parts and their functions, and finally remarked:

"It's coming, sure."

"What do you refer to?" asked Harvey.

"The day when those things will be as common as automobiles and bicycles. If I don't peg out in the next ten years, I expect to own one myself."

"I certainly hope so, for you will get great pleasure from it."

"Not to mention a broken neck or arm or leg," he remarked with a chuckle. "Now I suppose you call this contrivance a biplane because it has double wings?"

"That is the reason."

"And it seems to me," he added, turning his head to one side and squinting, "the length is a little greater from the nose of the forward rudder to the end of the tail than between the wing tips?"

"You are correct again; there is a difference of about two feet."

"The wings are curved a bit; I have read that that shape is better than the flat form to support you in air."

"Experiments have proved it so."

"And this stuff," he continued, touching his forefinger to the taut covering of one of the wings, "is rubberized linen?"

"It is with our machine, though some aviators prefer other material."

"Spruce seems to be the chief wood in your biplane."

"Because of its lightness and strength."

"The horizontal rudder in front must be used in ascending and descending and the two vertical ones at the rear for steering your course. I should judge," he said, scrutinizing the motor, "that your engine has about sixty-horse power."

"You hit it exactly; I am astonished by your knowledge."

"It all comes from remembering what I read. And the wing tips are the ailerons, and the engine weighs about three hundred pounds."

"A trifle less, the whole weight of the aeroplane being eight hundred pounds."

"Your propeller is made of black walnut, and has eight laminations, and when under full headway revolves more than a thousand times a minute."

"See here," said Harvey; "don't say you haven't examined aeroplanes before."

"As I told you, I never saw one until now, but what's the use of reading anything unless you keep it in your memory? That's my principle."

CHAPTER VI.
WORKING FOR DINNER.

Further conversation justified the astonishment of Harvey Hamilton. The countryman, who gave his name as Abisha Wharton, showed a knowledge of aviation and heavier-than-air machines such as few amateurs possess. In the midst of his bright remarks he abruptly checked himself.

"What time is it?"

Harvey glanced at the little watch on his wrist.

"Twenty minutes of six."

"You two will take supper with me."

Bohunkus Johnson, who had been silently listening while the three were standing, heaved an enormous sigh.

"Dat's what I'se been waitin' to hear mentioned eber since we landed; yas, we'll take supper wid yo'; I neber was so hungry in my life."

"I appreciate your kindness, which I accept on condition that we pay you or your wife for it. We have started on an outing, and that is our rule."

"I didn't have that in mind when I spoke, but if you insist on giving the old lady a little tip, we sha'n't quarrel; leastways I know she won't."

"That is settled then. Now I should like to hire you to do me a favor. I don't suppose you keep gasoline in your home?"

"Never had a drop; we use only candles and such light as the fire on the hearth gives."

"How near is there a store where we can buy the stuff?"

"I suppose Peters has it, for he sells everything from a toothpick to a folding bed. He keeps the main store at Darbytown, two miles away. I drive there nearly every day."

"Will you do so now, and buy me ten gallons of gasoline and two gallons of cylinder oil?"

"I don't see why I shouldn't; certainly I'll do it. Do you want it right off?"

"Can you go to town and back before dark?"

"My horse isn't noted for his swiftness," replied Abisha with a grin, "but I can come purty nigh making it, if I start now."

"Dat's a good idee; while yo's gone, Harv and me can put ourselves outside ob dat supper dat yo' remarked about."

Harvey's first thought was to accompany his new friend to the village, but when he saw the rickety animal and the dilapidated wagon to which he was soon harnessed, he forebore out of consideration for the brute. Besides, it looked as if he was likely to fail with the task. Accordingly, our young friend handed a five-dollar bill to his host and repeated his instructions. Then he and Bohunkus sauntered to the rude porch, where Mrs. Wharton came forth at the call of her husband, and was introduced to the visitors, whose names were given by Harvey. She promised that the evening meal should suit them and passed inside to look after its preparation.

The winding wagon road was well marked, and Abisha Wharton, seated in the front of his rattling vehicle, struck his bony horse so smart a blow that the animal broke into a loping trot, and speedily passed from sight among the trees in the direction of Darbytown. Harvey and Bohunkus, having nothing to hold their attention, strolled to the woodpile and sat down on one of the small logs lying there, awaiting cutting into proper length and size for the old-fashioned stove in the kitchen. A few minutes later the wife came out and gathered all that was ready for use. As she straightened up, she remarked with a sniff:

"That Abisha Wharton is too lazy ever to cut 'nough wood to last a day; all he keers about is to smoke his pipe, or fish, or read his papers and books."

When she had gone in, Harvey said to his companion:

"We haven't anything to do for an hour or so; let's make ourselves useful."

"I'm agreeable," replied Bohunkus, lifting one of the heavy pieces and depositing it in the two X's which formed the wood horse. The saw lay near and was fairly sharp. The colored youth was powerful and had good wind. He bent to work with a vigor that soon severed the piece in the middle. He immediately picked up another to subject it to the same process, while Harvey swung the rather dull axe and split the wood for the stove. It was all clean white hickory, with so straight a grain that a slight blow caused it to break apart. The work was light and Harvey offered to relieve his companion at the saw.

"Don't bodder me; dis am fun; besides," added Bohunkus, "I cac'late to make it up when I git at de supper table; I tell yo', Harv, yo'll hab to gib dat lady a big tip."

"I certainly shall if I wish to save her from losing on you."

For nearly an hour the two wrought without stopping to rest. By that time, most of the wood was cut and heaped into a sightly pile. The odor of the hickory was fragrant, and it made a pretty sight, besides which we all know that it has hardly a superior for fuel, unless it be applewood.

By and by the woman of the house came to the door and looked at the two boys. She was delighted, for she saw enough wood ready cut for the stove to last her for a week at least. Bohunkus was bending over the saw horse with one knee on the stick, while a tiny stream of grains shot out above and below, keeping time with the motion of the implement, and Harvey swung the axe aloft with an effect that kept the respective tasks equal. Gazing at them for a moment, the housewife called:

"Supper's waiting!"

"So am I!" replied Bohunkus, who, having a stick partly sawn in two worked with such energy that the projecting end quickly fell to the ground. Harvey would not allow him to leave until the pieces were split and piled upon the others.

"Now let us each carry in an armful."

They loaded themselves, and Harvey led the way into the house, where the smiling woman directed them to the kitchen. There being no box they dumped the wood upon the floor, then seated themselves at the table, and she waited upon them.

Despite her untidy appearance, Mrs. Wharton gave them an abundant and well-cooked meal, to which it need not be said both did justice. They were blessed with good appetites, Bohunkus especially being noted at home for his capacity in that line. They pleased the hostess by their compliments, but more so by their enjoyment of the meal.

It was a mild, balmy night, and at the suggestion of the woman they carried their stools outside and sat in front of the house and on the edge of the clearing, to await the return of the master of the household. Sooner than they expected, they heard the rattle of the wheels and the sound of his voice, as he urged his tired animal onward. It took but a few minutes for him to unfasten, water and lead him to the stable. Then the man came forward and greeted his friends.

"How did you make out?" asked Harvey.

"I got what I went after, of course; the gasoline and oil are in the wagon, and there's about three dollars coming to you."

"Which you will keep," replied Harvey. "We have finished an excellent meal and shall wait here for you if you don't mind."

"I'm agreeable to anything," remarked the man, as he slouched inside, where by the light of a candle he ate the evening meal with his wife. Our friends could not help hearing what she said, for she had a sharp voice and spoke in a high key. She berated him for his shiftlessness and declared he ought to be ashamed to allow two strangers to saw and split the wood which had too long awaited his attention. She made other observations that it is not worth while to repeat, but evidently the man was used to nagging, for it did not affect his appetite and he only grunted now and then by way of reply or to signify that he heard.

When Abisha brought out his chair and lighted his corncob pipe, it was fully dark. The night was without a moon, and the sky had so clouded that only here and there a twinkling star showed.

"Do you ever fly at night?" asked their host.

"We have never done so," replied Harvey, "because there is nothing to be gained and it is dangerous."

"Why dangerous?"

"We can't carry enough gasoline to keep us in the air more than two hours, and it is a risky thing to land in the darkness. If I hadn't caught sight of this open space, it would have gone hard with us even when the sun was shining."

"It's a wonderful discovery," repeated Wharton, as if speaking with himself, "but a lot of improvements will have to be made. One of them is to carry more gasoline or find some stuff that will serve better. How long has anyone been able to sail with an aeroplane without landing?"

"I believe the record is something like five hours."

"In two or three years or less time, they will keep aloft for a day or more. They'll have to do it in order to cross the Atlantic."

"There is little prospect of ever doing that."

"Wellman tried it in a balloon, but was not able to make more than a start."

"I agree with you that the day is not distant when the Atlantic will be crossed as regularly by heavier-than-air machines as it is by the Mauretania and Lusitania, but in the meantime we have got to make many improvements; that of carrying enough fuel being the most important."

At this point Bohunkus felt that an observation was due from him.

"Humph! it's easy 'nough to fix dat."

"How?"

"Hab reg'lar gasumline stations all de way 'cross de ocean, so dat anyone can stop and load up when he wants to."

"How would you keep the stations in place?" gravely inquired Wharton.

"Anchor 'em, ob course."

"But the ocean is several miles in depth in many portions."

"What ob dat? Can't you make chains or ropes dat long? Seems to me some folks is mighty dumb."

"I've noticed that myself," remarked the host without a smile. Failing to catch the drift of his comment, Bohunkus held his peace for the next few minutes, but in the middle of a remark by his companion, he suddenly leaped to his feet with the gasping question:

"What's dat?"

CHAPTER VII.
THE DRAGON OF THE SKIES.

The others had seen the same object which so startled Bohunkus. Several hundred feet up in the air and slightly to the north, the gleam of a red light showed. It was moving slowly in the direction of the three, all of whom were standing and studying it with wondering curiosity. It was as if some aerial wanderer was flourishing a danger lantern through the realms of space.

"What can it be?" asked Abisha Wharton in an awed voice.

Not knowing the proper answer, Harvey Hamilton held his peace, but Bohunkus had an explanation ready.

"It am de comet!" he exclaimed, having in mind the celestial visitor named in honor of Halley the astronomer, over which the world had been stirred a short time before; "it hab broke loose and is gwine to hit de airth; we'd better dodge."

And he plunged into the house, where the wife had lighted a candle and set it on the table in the front room. The others left him to his own devices while they kept their eyes on the mysterious visitant to the upper world.

They saw that the light was moving in a circle a hundred feet in diameter, and gradually descending. Whatever connection anything else had with it was invisible in the gloom. If the peculiar motion continued, it must come down in the clearing where Harvey's biplane had settled to rest some time before.

Suddenly a fanlike stream of light shot out from a point directly above the crimson glow. It darted here and there, whisked over the small plain, flitted above the treetops and then flashed into the faces of the two persons who were standing side by side.

"It's another aeroplane!" cried Harvey; "it carries a searchlight and the man is hunting a spot to land."

At this juncture, Bohunkus's curiosity got the better of him. He came timidly to the open door and peeped out.

"Hab it struck yet?" he asked; "it'll be mighty bad when it swipes yo' alongside de head. Better come in here——"

At that instant the blinding ray hit the dusky youth in the face, and with another gasp of affright, he dashed to the farthest corner of the room, where he cowered in trembling expectancy.

A FANLIKE STREAM OF LIGHT SHOT OUT.

The couple outside were too much absorbed in what they saw to give heed to him.

"You're right," said Wharton; "it's an aeroplane and the aviator means to alight."

The searchlight continued darting here and there, but the spreading glow finally settled upon the ground near where the biplane stood silent and motionless.

"It is unaccountable that it makes no noise. Look!"

The aviator now demonstrated that he was an expert in the management of his machine. He oscillated downward, zig-zagging to the right and left, until he gently touched the earth and the wheels running a short distance settled to rest. The searchlight flitted toward different points several times and then was abruptly extinguished. Harvey and Wharton walked across the ground toward the machine. Before they reached it, they made out the dim forms of a monoplane and a man standing beside it. To the youth he was the tallest and slimmest person he had ever seen. His stature must have been six and a half feet and in common language he was as thin as a rail. He had observed the approach of the two and silently awaited them.

"Good evening!" saluted Harvey, who was slightly in advance of his companion.

"How do you do, sir?"

The voice would have won an engagement for the owner as the basso profundo in an opera troupe. It was like the muttering of thunder, and as Abisha Wharton expressed it, seemed to come from his shoes.

Since Wharton left it to his young friend to do the honors, Harvey, pausing a few paces away, exerted himself to play the host.

"I see that your machine is a monoplane; you seem to have it under good control."

"Why shouldn't I? I made every part of it."

"Even to the searchlight?"

"Of course; is that biplane yours?"

"It is; we landed several hours ago, having been kindly furnished a meal and lodgings for the night. I presume you will keep us company; my friend here, I am sure, will be glad to do what he can for you."

"Kerrect," added Wharton; "you're as welcome as the flowers in spring."

"Don't you travel by night?" asked the visitor, ignoring the invitation.

"Not when I can avoid it; it is too risky to land in the darkness."

"Night is the favorite period with me."

"But you can't keep in the air all the time."

"What do you know about it, young man?" asked the other in his sepulchral tones; "I don't expect to make a landing till after sunrise to-morrow."

"I never heard of such a thing."

"There are lots of things you never heard of; I built this monoplane, without help from any one; it embodies a number of new principles, one of which is the ability to keep in the air for twelve hours without renewing the gasoline; I mix a certain chemical with that fluid which increases its power tenfold; I shall not rest until it is multiplied a hundred times."

"You have an invention that will make you wealthier than Carnegie or Rockefeller."

"I'm not seeking wealth," said the other sourly, as if not pleased with the suggestion; "there are better things in life than riches."

"All the same, it's mighty pleasant to have them," replied Harvey, nettled as much by the manner as by the words of the stranger.

"See here," interposed the hospitable Wharton; "we are keeping you standing——"

"There is no compulsion about it, sir; I am doing what pleases me best."

"Will you walk into my house and have something to eat? There isn't much style about us, but my wife will give you a good cup of coffee and some corn bread and fried chicken."

"I'll go to your house, but I'll not eat for I'm not hungry."

Wharton led the way to the porch. Harvey, who was curious to learn more of this strange individual, deftly placed his chair so that the rays from the candle fell through the open window upon him. In obedience to the youth's order, Bohunkus brought out a fourth stool, so that all were seated, the woman of the house remaining inside and attending to her duties, as if she felt no interest in what was going on.

The negro sat close to his companion and huskily whispered:

"Am he de feller dat rid down on de comet?"

"Bunk, the best thing you can do is to keep still and listen; our conversation is likely to be above your head."

"Jest like de comet; all right; I ain't saying nuffin."

A part of the yellow rays touched Harvey, and the stranger turned and scrutinized him as if impelled by curiosity similar to that of the youth. The movement revealed the visitor's face plainly, and it may be said it was in keeping with the impression he had already made. He wore a motorman's cap, and a long, linen duster, buttoned to the chin and reaching downward to his slim tan shoes. What clothing was within this envelope was out of sight.

The face was long and covered with a grizzled beard that reached well down on his breast. He had removed his buckskin gloves, crossed his legs, and placed one of the hand coverings in his lap, while he loosely grasped the other and idly flipped the first with it as he talked.

But his eyes were the most striking feature of the remarkable man. They were overhung by shaggy brows, were of a piercing black color, and glowed as if with fire. Their startling glare caused a sudden suspicion in the mind of Harvey Hamilton that the man was partially insane. At least, he must be the curious individual best described by the word "crank," one whom much study and research had made mad. As is well known, such a person often succeeds in hiding his affliction from his friends, or gains the reputation of being simply eccentric.

"What is your name and why are you here?" he abruptly asked, still looking in the face of Harvey, who said he lived at Mootsport, something more than a hundred miles distant.

"I have started on an outing with my colored friend, without any particular destination in view; when we have had enough sport, we shall return. Who are you?" queried the youth, feeling warranted in asking a few equally pointed questions.

"My name is Milo Morgan; I have no special home, but stop where the notion takes me; my business is invention, as it relates to the aeroplane."

"May I ask what improvements you have made, Professor?"

He hesitated a moment as if uncertain what to reply.

"Not half as many as I am sure of making in the near future. The rigging of a searchlight cannot be called an invention, for it has long been in common use on warships and others, and all aeroplanes are supplied with electricity. I have rigged up a wireless telegraph, so as to pick out messages from the air; I have succeeded in compounding a fluid which as I told you is ten times stronger than gasoline; I run without noise, and my uplifter will carry me vertically upward, as high as I care to go."

"I should think you were blamed near the limit," suggested Abisha Wharton, profoundly interested in what the Professor was saying.

"I have only begun; and I intend to justify the name of my monoplane."

"I didn't hear it."

"Because I haven't spoken it, but when you have a daylight view of my machine you will see the name painted on the under side of the wings, 'The Dragon of the Skies.'"

This was said with so much solemnity that Harvey had hard work to hide his smile. He no longer doubted that he was talking with a crank.

"Do you mind telling me what is the great object you have in view?"

"It is to build a machine that will keep afloat and travel at an average speed of sixty miles an hour,—probably greater. That will enable me to cross the Atlantic in a little more than two days and I shall have no difficulty in sailing to Asia or Africa."

CHAPTER VIII.
THE PROFESSOR TALKS ON AVIATION.

The last remark of Professor Morgan threw Bohunkus Johnson into a state of excitement. He had obeyed Harvey and remained mute during the conversation, but he now addressed the visitor directly:

"Did yo' say Afriky, boss?"

The man looked in his direction and nodded his head.

"That's what I said, sir."

"Dat's where my fader libs."

Harvey felt it his duty to explain:

"My colored friend claims to be the son of a distinguished African chief, whom he hopes to visit some day."

"What is the name of the chief?" asked the Professor.

"His given name is the same as his; the full name is Bohunkus Foozleum."

"I can't say I ever heard of him," remarked the Professor without cracking a smile.

"I sent him a letter a month ago, in de care ob Colonel Roosevelt and it's 'bout time I got an answer. I'm sure de Colonel will call on him while he's hunting in Afriky."

"Well, when my machine is perfected, I'll take you with me and it sha'n't cost you a penny," said Professor Morgan.

Bohunkus chuckled with delight and settled down to listen. The visitor now ignored him and addressed the others.

"Aviation is the theme that fills nearly all minds and it is daily growing in importance. The possibilities are boundless; it will revolutionize travel, social life and the methods of warfare. It will render the destruction of life and property so appallingly easy that no nation will dare array itself against another. You and I are likely to see that day when:—

"'The war drum throbs no longer and the battle flags are furled

O'er the parliament of nations, o'er a reunited world.'

"We can remember the universality of the bicycle; then came, and it stays with us, the automobile, and now it is the aeroplane. The day is near when there will be numberless routes established between cities and countries and when the ocean will be crossed east and west by a procession of heavier-than-air machines, and every family will have its hangar and its occupant awaiting the wish of the owner."

The Professor showed a disposition to quiz the young aviator, who met him as best he could, though sensible of his lack of knowledge as compared with one who had given so much thought and experimentation to it.

"Naturally," said he, "men's first ideas were of using wings as birds do, but it would take a Samson or a Hercules to put forth the necessary strength. But it has been tried times without number. I think the ancient Greeks wove many romantic tales of aerial flights—"

The Professor paused and Harvey accepted the invitation:

"Such as Daedalus and Icarus, who were said to have flown to the sun and back again. The Greek Achytus made a dove of wood, driven by heated air, and one of his countrymen constructed a brass fly which kept above the ground for some minutes."

"Do you recall what aviator first came to grief?"

"'Simon the Magician,' who during the reign of the emperor Nero made a short flight before a Roman crowd but tumbled to death, as did a good many during the Middle Ages."

"The Chinese were centuries ahead of the rest of the world in the use of the mariner's compass, printing, gunpowder and the flying of kites. There are authentic records of balloon flights in the fourteenth century, and a hundred years later discoveries were made of which present aviators have taken advantage. You have learned that although America was visited a thousand years ago and even earlier by white men, the glory of the discovery is given to Christopher Columbus. So the credit of the first real step in aviation belongs to two Frenchmen. Can you help me to recall their names?"

"I don't think you need any help," laughed Harvey, who saw the drift of his friend's quizzing, "but the men you have in mind were Joseph and Etienne Montgolfier, who lived at Annonay, about forty miles from Lyons."

"What was their idea of aerostation?"

"They learned from many experiments that a light globe filled with hot air will rise because its weight is less than the surrounding atmosphere, just as a cork or bit of pine comes to the surface of water. They made a globular ball, thirty-five feet in diameter, of varnished silk, and in June, 1783, in the presence of an immense crowd at Annonay built a fire under the mouth on the lower side. Soon after when the ropes were loosened, the balloon mounted upward for more than a mile, then was carried to one side by a current of air and as the vapor within cooled, came gently down to earth again.

"The incident caused a sensation and Paris subscribed money for manufacturing hydrogen, a very buoyant gas to take the place of hot air. The brothers sent up such a balloon in Paris in the latter part of August. It sailed aloft for half a mile, finally drifted out of sight and came down fifteen miles from the starting point."

"Did it carry any passenger?" asked the Professor.

"No; the time had not come for that venture, but soon after the brothers sent up a second hot air balloon at Versailles, in the presence of the king and queen. A wicker cage was suspended below and in it were a duck, a rooster and a sheep, all of which showed less excitement than the cheering thousands. It rose about a fourth of a mile, and eight minutes after leaving the ground descended two miles away."

"Who was the first man to go up in a balloon?" asked Abisha Wharton.

"I don't remember his name; can you tell me, Professor?"

"Pilatre de Rozier, whose ascent was made on the 15th of October, 1783, in an oval balloon constructed by the Montgolfiers. It was not quite fifty feet in diameter and half again as high. A circular wicker basket was suspended beneath, and under the neck of the balloon in the center was an iron grate or brazier supported by chains, the whole structure weighing sixteen hundred pounds. M. de Rozier fed the flames with straw and wood and thus kept the air sufficiently heated to lift him eighty-four feet, where held by ropes, the balloon remained suspended for four and a half minutes and then gently came back to earth.

"This incident blazed the way for successful aerostation. M. de Rozier accomplished higher and more durable ascents and occasionally took a passenger with him. We must remember, however, that in all these instances, the balloon was restrained by ropes and could not wander off. The aeronauts chafed under such restriction, and on November 21, 1783, M. de Rozier and the Marquis d'Arlandes cut loose from the earth in front of a royal palace in the Bois de Boulogne, it being the first time such a thing was ever done. The ascent lasted not quite half an hour, when the aeronauts came safely down in a field five miles distant from the starting point." [1]

1. It is well to bear the following distinctions in mind: aerostation is the art of flying in a balloon; when the balloon is equipped with motor and propellers so as to be navigable, it is dirigible; an aerocar is any kind of a flying machine; an aeronaut is any one who navigates the air in a balloon; an aeroplane is a flying machine which is heavier than air; a monoplane is a one-planed and a biplane a two-planed flying machine; a triplane consists of three superposed planes; a quadruplane of four planes; airmen are either aeronauts or aviators; aviation is the art of flying in an aeroplane and an aviator is one who so flies; aeronef is an aeroplane as defined by International Congress; a hangar corresponds to a garage for an automobile; ornithopter is a heavier-than-air machine, with wings upon which it depends for support and propulsion; petrol is the European name for gasoline.

CHAPTER IX.
THE PROFESSOR TALKS ON AVIATION (Continued.)

Professor Morgan continued: "Thus far the aeronauts had used hot air with which to make their ascents, but the fire under the balloon was always dangerous and more than one fatal accident resulted therefrom. Hydrogen gas was far better, but more costly. Public subscriptions enabled two brothers named Robert, assisted by M. Charles, to construct a spherical balloon, twenty-eight feet in diameter, the silk envelope being covered with varnish, and the upper half inclosed in a network which supported a hoop that encircled the middle of the sphere. A boat-like structure dangled a few feet below the mouth, and was attached to the hoop, while a safety valve at the apex prevented bursting through expansion of the gas as the balloon climbed the sky.

"This structure was inflated with hydrogen gas in the Garden of the Tuileries, Paris, on the first of December, 1783. M. Charles and one of the Roberts seated themselves in the car, provided with extra clothing, provisions, sand bags for ballast, a barometer and a thermometer, and gave the word to let go. The balloon soared swiftly, the aeronauts waving hands and hats in response to the cheers of the multitudes below. The ascent was a success in every respect. Having drifted thirty miles from Paris, the balloon safely descended near Nesle. There was so much gas left that the enthusiastic M. Charles decided to go up again, after parting with his companion. He climbed nine thousand feet and then by the dexterous use of his ballast came to earth again without the least jar.

"The impulse thus given to ballooning spread to other countries and it would be idle to attempt any record of their efforts. It may be said that for nearly a hundred years little or no progress was made in aerostation. Then came the second stage, the construction of dirigible or manageable balloons. All the structures which had hitherto left the earth were wholly under control of air currents, as much as a chip of wood is under the control of the stream into which it is flung. People began to experiment with a view of directing the course of the ships of the sky. While it was impossible to make headway against a gale or strong wind, it seemed that the aeronaut ought to be able to overcome a moderate breeze. The first attempt was by means of oars and a rudder, but nothing was accomplished until 1852, when Giffard used a small engine, but the difficulty of constructing a light motor of sufficient power checked all progress for awhile. It could not do so for long, however, as the inventive genius of mankind was at work and would not pause until satisfied. One of Giffard's stupendous ideas was a balloon more than a third of a mile long with an engine weighing thirty tons, but the magnitude and expense involved were too vast to be considered.

"It would be tedious to follow the various steps in dirigible ballooning. It was not until 1882, that the Tissandier brothers, Gilbert and Albert—Frenchmen—built a dirigible cigar-shaped balloon substantially on the old lines, but it could not be made to travel more than five miles an hour in a dead calm, and was helpless in a moderate wind. None the less their attempts marked an epoch, for they introduced an electric motor. The 'La France,' when constructed some time later, was a hundred and sixty-five feet long, twenty-seven feet at its greatest diameter, and had a capacity of sixty-six thousand cubic feet. Many changes and improvements followed and an ascent was made in August, 1884, during which the balloon traveled two and a half miles, turned round and came back in the face of a gentle breeze to its starting point, the whole time in the air being less than half an hour. This was the first exploit of that nature.

"But," added the Professor, "I am talking too much about dirigible ballooning, for our chief interest does not lie there. I am sure you have read of the Schwartz aluminum dirigible; Santos-Dumont and his brilliant performances with his fourteen airships; Roze's double airship, and Count Zeppelin's splendid successes with his colossal dirigibles.

"We have dealt only with structures that were lighter than air. The wonderful field that has opened before us and into which thousands are crowding, with every day bringing new and startling achievements, is that of the heavier-than-air machines. In other words, we have learned to become air men and to fly as the birds fly.

"Success was sure to come sooner or later, and when it did come every one wondered why it was so late, since the principles are so simple that a child can understand them. Otto Lilienthal, after long study and experimentation, published in Berlin in 1889, as one of the results of his labors, the discovery that arched surfaces driven against the wind have a strong tendency to rise. Then he demonstrated by personal experiments that a beginning must be made by 'gliding' through the air in order to learn to balance one's self. He piled up a lot of dirt fifty feet high, and from its summit made a number of starts, succeeding so well that he tried a small motor to help flap his wings. Sad to say, an error of adjustment caused the machine to turn over in August, 1896, and he was killed.

"Percy S. Pilcher of England experimented for several years along the same lines and used the method of a kite by employing men to run with a rope against the wind, but he was destined to become another martyr, for he was fatally injured one day by a fall. Chanute and Herring of Chicago taught us a good deal about gliders. Herring used a motor driven by compressed air and had two plane surfaces for his apparatus, but his motor was too weak to sustain him for more than a few minutes."

"Professor," said Wharton, "I have often heard of the Hargrave kite; why do folks call it that name?"

"You mean the box pattern, made of calico stretched over redwood frames. They are the invention of Lawrence Hargrave of Sydney, Australia. He attached a sling seat to one and connected three above it. A brisk wind showed a lift of more than two hundred pounds, and he made a number of ascents, the kites preserving their stability most satisfactorily.

"Of course you do not need to be told anything about Orville and Wilbur Wright of Dayton, Ohio. These plucky and persevering fellows experimented for years in the effort to overcome obstacles that had baffled inventors for centuries. Among the problems they solved were whether stability is most effectively gained by shifting the center of gravity, or by a special steering device, and what the power of a rudder is when fixed in front of a machine. They decided that in gliding experiments it is best for the aviator to lie in a horizontal position; that a vertical rudder in the rear of a machine is preferable in order to turn to the right or left, and a horizontal rudder or small plane in front is the most effective device for guiding the aeroplane up or down."

The Professor was in the middle of his interesting talk, when he abruptly paused and came to his feet.

"I've stayed longer than I intended," said he; "I must bid you good night. If it won't be too much trouble to your wife I shall be glad to drink a cup of coffee."

"No trouble at all," replied Abisha Wharton springing from his stool; "won't you eat something?"

"I don't need it."

The three walked through the open door into the larger room where the wife was sitting. Bohunkus was leaning back against the front of the house sound asleep, as he had been for some minutes. No one disturbed him. The woman had heard the words of the visitor, and quickly brought in a big coffee pot from which she poured a brimming cup, placing some milk and sugar on the table. The Professor had not yet thanked any one for the proffers made him and he did not do so now, but standing erect, with his cap almost touching the ceiling, he drank, smacked his thin lips and remarked that the refreshment was good.

Standing thus clearly disclosed in the candle-light, the Professor impressed Harvey Hamilton more than before. He was as straight as an arrow and his piercing black eyes had a gleam that must have possessed hypnotic power. In fact the woman showed so much restlessness under his glances that she made a pretext for leaving the room and remained out of sight until he departed. He did not offer to pay his host and still forgot to acknowledge by word the kindnesses shown him.

Harvey and Abisha accompanied him on his brief walk across the little plain to where his machine was waiting. Without any preliminaries such as testing the wires, levers, framework and different parts of the apparatus, he seated himself.

"Now," he said in his thunderous bass, "note the action of my uplifter."

This contrivance was simply a horizontal propeller under the machine, which being set revolving with great rapidity hoisted it gently from the ground and as straight upward as a cannon shot fired at the zenith. It was easy to understand the principle of the action, but not of some of the other performances of the eccentric inventor. When the aerocar was well off the earth, the regular propeller in front began work and the uplifter became motionless.

All this time only a faint humming noise was noticeable, but in a few minutes that became inaudible. Professor Morgan was swallowed up in the darkness and speedily vanished, for he made no use of his searchlight. He must have been half a mile to the northward when he let off a rocket. Ordinary prudence on account of sparks probably caused him to send it sideways. It formed a striking picture,—this germination as it were of a blazing object in mid air, which shot away with arrowy swiftness in a graceful parabola that curved downward, and when about half way to the ground burst into a myriad of dazzling sparks of different hues that were quickly lost in the gloom.

The two spectators waited and gazed in silence, but saw nothing more and returned to their seats in front of the cabin.

"Strange man," said Harvey, "I wonder whether we shall ever see him again."

"I don't think there is much chance of my meeting him, but you may bump against him some time when you are cruising overhead."

"That seems hardly likely, for the field is too big."

And yet Harvey Hamilton and Professor Milo Morgan were destined to meet sooner than either suspected and in circumstances of which neither could have dreamed.

Wharton refilled his corncob pipe and puffed with deliberate enjoyment.

"What do you think of him, Mr. Hamilton?" he finally asked.

"He's wonderfully well informed about aviation, but is cranky."

"He's more than that."

"What do you mean?"

"He's plumb crazy."

"You wouldn't think so from his conversation; no one can talk better than he."

"But his eyes! They gave him dead away; I'm glad he didn't stay all night."

"What difference could that make?"

"More'n likely he would have got up and killed us all while we were asleep."

Harvey laughed.

"While he isn't the sort of companion I should fancy, I'm sure he is not that kind of a lunatic. The chances are that he will lose his life through some of his experiments in aviation, the same as those we talked about."

"Shall we say anything to Bohunkus about the man being off his base?" asked Wharton, as if in doubt regarding his duty in the circumstances.

"It isn't worth while; nothing can be gained by doing so."

And in reaching this decision, Harvey Hamilton made a grand mistake, as he was fated to learn before many days. It would have been a fortunate thing, too, had the colored youth kept awake during this chat, but it was not so to be.

As the night advanced, the host told his guest he was at liberty to retire whenever agreeable. The couple had a sleeping room upstairs, and not being well provided for company, a blanket was spread on the floor in the lower front room. Bohunkus was still unconscious, his cap having fallen at his feet. Harvey reached over and shook his shoulder.

"Come, Bunk, it's time to go to bed—excuse me!"

Although the action was gentle, it destroyed the sleeper's center of gravity, and he and the stool tumbled over on the floor. Even then, he was only partially awakened and mumbled a wish that folks would stay on their own side of the bed, as he climbed unsteadily to his feet.

The weather was so mild that there was no discomfort in occupying a room whose windows and door were open. With the aid of the candle, Bohunkus stumbled to the blanket in the corner, pitched down upon it and the next minute was slumbering as soundly as when his stool tipped over with him. He and Harvey had laid aside their heavy coats before they sawed and split the supply of wood, and the single blanket gave them all the protection they needed. Thus the two lay down to pleasant dreams.

CHAPTER X.
THE FLYING BOYS CONTINUE THEIR JOURNEY.

The morning dawned clear, mild and bright. Harvey and Bohunkus were astir at an early hour and filled the tank with gasoline and replenished the supply of oil. An examination of the aeroplane was made and every wire, brace, lever and appurtenance found, so far as could be judged, in perfect condition. The two went back to the house where an excellent meal was awaiting them. Harvey slipped so liberal a fee into the hands of the woman that she was delighted and showed it to her husband, who grinned appreciatively. It may be said that he earned the extra pay through a valuable suggestion to the aviator,—one that was effective and so simple that it was strange it had not been thought of before.

"You tell me," said Abisha, "that when one of them things is ready to start on its flight, you hold it until the propeller has got its grip and then let it go with a jump."

"Something like that is the practice."

"When there's only two of you, how do you manage it?"

"The only way is to start the thing, with Bunk in his seat; I run alongside for a few steps and spring into my seat."

"You might slip and let the aeroplane get away from you. Then Bunk would be thrown out on his head."

"He wouldn't be hurt if he landed that way," replied Harvey with a laugh, "but he might alight on his shins and that would be bad."

"Let me show you a better plan."

Abisha strode to the woodpile and came back with a long, strong stick. He set one end in the ground, with the upper inclined against the footboard. The prop thus gained held the biplane immovable before a strong push.

"Let her shove all she wants to," explained the man, "and when you're ready, kick the stick aside."

"The scheme could not be better," said Harvey admiringly, as he made sure that the point in contact with the machine could not injure it. He seated himself and Abisha swung the propeller around; the engine instantly responded with its deafening roar and a powerful thrust was exerted against the prop. In a few minutes, the youth leaned over, grasped the stick and swung it aside. The machine made a bound like a runner starting on a race, spun over the ground for a hundred feet or more, and then in obedience to the upturned rudder in front, leaped clear of the ground. She was off.

Harvey glanced back. In the door was the smiling housewife, with her husband on the spot where he stood when the flight began. He waved his hand in salutation and the two aviators responded.

This is a good place in which to give the explanation that must be made in order to understand how it came about that these two youths were so far from home, and engaged upon the outing that was destined to prove the most memorable in the life at least of one of them.

Harvey Hamilton was the son of a wealthy merchant, whose business took him to New York every week-day morning. The youth was preparing to enter Princeton University, and his elder brother Dick was a student in Yale. In the beginning of the summer the family separated, each member indulging his or her taste in the way of vacation, with the parent glad to pay the bills. The mother and daughter Mildred went to the White Mountains, Dick to the Adirondacks with a party of students, while Harvey and his father took a jaunt through a part of Europe, sailing home from Naples on the Duca degli Abruzzi. Wife and daughter, knowing when they were due, were at home to meet them. Dick was still in the mountains, from which he wrote the most glowing accounts of his life in camp and conquests of the gamy trout that are still to be found in the cool streams.

On the homeward passage, Harvey and his father were lucky enough to meet the noted German aviator, Ostrom Sperbeck, of whom we have heard already.

Mr. Hamilton explained to the Professor that his son Harvey with the assistance of the colored youth, who was "bound out" to a neighbor, were at work on an aeroplane with which they hoped to fly, but the Professor warned them against it.

"It is too dangerous; some of the best aviators have lost their lives and you know that one of the Wright brothers came within a hair of being killed. Encourage your son, if you wish, in the sport, for those who are boys to-day are the ones that will make the greatest discoveries and advances in aviation, but do not let him take any risks that can be avoided. Buy him a first-class machine and forbid him to use any other."

Mr. Hamilton was impressed with the advice and acted upon it.

Bohunkus Johnson was as ardent as his young friend, but, lacking his mental brightness, was not given charge of the aeroplane, though promised a chance of trying his hand later on.

So much having been told, it will be understood how on a pleasant summer day, Harvey and Bohunkus started on their outing, with permission to be gone several weeks, though their expectation was to return in the course of ten days or so.

Several facts will be borne in mind. Nothing not deemed absolutely necessary was taken with the aviators. Inasmuch as they could not stay more than two hours in the air, without replenishing their supply of fuel, they carried no food, nor were any weapons taken along, for it was not probable they would ever need anything of the kind. Although Harvey headed toward a spur of the Alleghany Mountains, with the object of relieving what promised to become a monotonous experience at times, it did not seem possible that they would ever run into personal danger from that cause. He carried a pair of binoculars held by a strap over one shoulder, for such an instrument was likely to prove useful in their voyages through the air.

Harvey ascended for a fourth of a mile, and Bohunkus shuddered at the thought of plunging again into the arctic regions, but his friend lowered the front rudder and they skimmed away on a level. The view was as entrancing as ever, with cities, towns, villages, scattered houses, stretches of wood and cultivated country, winding streams, puffing engines pulling trains that looked like insignificant toys, and the gleam of what seemed to be a lake of several miles area in the distance. The wanderer through the finest picture galleries in Europe can become sated with the numberless master-pieces, and wonderful as was the unfolding panorama, the youths grew tired of its splendid sameness. When they gazed at the earth it was without any clear impression of what they saw.

Far to the westward loomed a mountain, the outlines showing a dim blue haze against the summer sky. Harvey had fixed the elevation in his mind before leaving home and, it was his intention to sail over the summit into the more unsettled country beyond. As near as he could judge the range was about twenty miles distant.

"I can easily make it in an hour," he reflected, "and not hurry."

He was traveling at a moderate pace, for he did not like to impose a strain upon the machine by pressing it to the limit. There was no call for hurry, and after clearing the elevation he could land at some town and buy what gasoline he needed. He shifted the course of the aeroplane slightly, and descended until within two or three hundred feet of the earth. There were no tall buildings to be avoided, and none of the trees that showed were lofty enough to interfere. Bohunkus sat in his usual seat, idly grasping the supports, for the progress was so smooth that he might have folded his arms without risk, always provided the aeroplane did not collide with any of the fierce aerial gyrations, which are so dangerous to aviators, because being invisible, no precaution can be taken against them.

Harvey slackened his speed still more, and coursed easily forward, crossed a winding creek, and was skimming toward a moderate stretch of woods, when he noticed a man standing on the margin and watching the aeroplane. The fact that he held a gun in one hand did not concern the youth, who, prompted by the spirit of mischief natural in one of his years, dropped still lower and headed for the man, as if he meant to crash into him.

The stranger, instead of turning about and dashing into the wood where he would have been safe from pursuit, suddenly raised his double-barreled shot gun and let fly with both charges. Nothing of the kind had been dreamed of, either by Harvey or his companion, and they were startled indeed when they heard the shot rattle through the wires and framework of the machine. One of the pellets nipped the cheek of Harvey and Bohunkus yelled,

"I'm shot all to pieces, Harv!"

Harvey turned his head in affright, but saw no evidence that the other had been harmed in the least. The man, seeing that his hasty aim had been ineffective, began hastily to reload his weapon with the evident purpose of doing execution next time.

CHAPTER XI.
FIRED ON.

Bohunkus Johnson was never so angry in his life and the resentment of Harvey Hamilton was equally intense. That a man should deliberately shoot at their machine without provocation more than a bit of harmless mischief, was beyond bearing. The colored youth stood up and shouted to his friend:

"I'm gwine to jump! I'll teach him sumfin!"

"Wait one moment," replied Harvey, as he shut off power and hastily dropped to earth. His momentum carried him several rods beyond the young man, who was still busy reloading his gun. Fortunately for our friends it was of the old-fashioned muzzle pattern, and required more time than the modern weapon. He roared with an oath:

"I'll larn you better than to go skyugling over the country and trying to scare folks to death. Jes' wait till I git my gun loaded agin!"

But neither Harvey nor Bohunkus had any intention of waiting. Before the machine came to a rest, the colored youth leaped to the ground and broke into a run for the man, who held his position.

"Yo's gwine to larn me something, am yo'? Wal, dis am de time to begin!"

"Sail into him, Bunk!" shouted Harvey, "and if you need any help, I'll give it!"

"All yo' got to do am to keep out ob dis bus'ness; I'm running dis funeral," replied the African, without shifting his gaze from the young farmer, who could not have been much older than Bohunkus. Not once did the latter check his pace, but dashed at full speed at the man. The instant he was within reach, he landed a blow that sent the other spinning backward, with his feet pointing upward and the weapon hurled from his grasp.

It was not a knockout, however, and the fellow was game. He bounded up again as if made of rubber, and charged in turn upon his assailant. Bohunkus had little "science," but he had been in many bouts, and was as strong as a bull. He braced himself to receive the attack, which came the next instant. A clenched fist landed on his jaw with a force that nearly carried him off his feet, and then the two went at it hammer and tongs, with no apparent advantage at first on either side.

Harvey, seeing that his machine was unharmed, watched the fight. Nothing would have suited him better than to take Bunk's place, for he had been taught boxing by a professional and he knew, though he might not have been so big or strong as his comrade, that he could readily vanquish the awkward but powerful fighter. Coolness, straight hitting and skilful parrying would do the business. He did not mean to stand idly by and see Bunk maltreated, but it would not be sportsmanlike to break in unless to stop the struggle.

The countryman was tough and wiry, and it is doubtful how the fight would have ended had it depended upon fists alone, but in one respect Bunk was much the other's superior. He was known as the best wrestler in the neighborhood of his home. When nearly a score of blows had been exchanged, the negro rushed in, grasped his antagonist about the waist, lifted him clear of the ground, and flung him on his back with a violence that it seemed must have jarred his teeth. Before he could spring to his feet again, Bunk was across his chest and evening up things in the most impressive style that can be imagined.

Suddenly the victim shouted at the top of his voice:

"Bill! Sam! Dick! Tom! Hurry up and part us afore we kill each other!"

This was a strange appeal and puzzled Harvey, who was disposed to think it was simply a bluff. The victim was too proud to beg for mercy, and tried to scare off his assailant. Harvey stepped forward, picked up the partially loaded gun from the ground, and with several quick stamps of his shoe so broke the two hammers that the weapon became useless for the time.

"That will prevent his using it against us," was the thought of our young friend, who again turned his attention to the combatants on the ground.

"Don't be too hard on him, Bunk; I guess he's had enough."

"Why doan' he holler ''nough!' den? dat's what I'm waitin' fur."

The victim had ceased his outcries, and was desperately trying to writhe free and roll off the burden, but his master couldn't be shaken from his perch.

"Why doan' yo' holler like a gemman oughter do when he's had 'nough? Holloa!"

When Harvey Hamilton thought the fellow was merely bluffing by his calls for help, he made a mistake. From out of the wood came running a man larger and older than any one of the three, and he was followed by a second, third and fourth,—all full grown, massive, muscular and each with fire in his eye. They had heard the cry of their comrade in extremity and made haste to come to his help.

Their arrival caused a change of program. Much as I like Bohunkus Johnson (and I trust that you, too, share the feeling), I am obliged to confess that like many of his race he had a tinge of yellow in his composition. So long as he held the upper hand, or so long as the fight was in doubt, he displayed courage, but the arrival of reinforcements threw him into a panic. He whisked off the prostrate figure, leaped to his feet and dashed at his highest speed into the woods. He ran like a person whose life was in danger, and the young man who had suffered at his hands sped after him, breathing threatenings and slaughter.

The new arrivals, who had been referred to as Bill, Sam, Dick and Tom, were evidently young farmers, none more than twenty-five years old. They had sturdy frames and could have given a good account of themselves in a physical struggle. They must have been mystified by what they saw, for the one who had dashed off in pursuit of Bohunkus had not paused to make explanation.

One fact was a vast relief to Harvey Hamilton: none of them carried a weapon, though it may be thought the quartet did not need anything of the kind in order to work their will with the slim active youth. The latter, with a quickness of resource which would have done credit to one older than himself, picked up the discarded shotgun at his feet, covering the lock as he did so with one hand in order to hide the harm it had suffered. So long as the others believed it sound and loaded, he could command the situation.

"Say, you," said the tallest of the quartette in a loud voice, "what's the meaning of this row? We don't exactly git the hang of things."

Facing the group and with his back toward the biplane, Harvey answered:

"Your friend had a misunderstanding with my friend, and it doesn't seem to be settled yet, though it looks as if yours had the advantage."

"What was the quarrel about?"

"Your friend—"

"That's Herb," interrupted the other speaker.

"Herb fired his gun at us without any cause."

"Yes; we heerd it; if he didn't have any cause, what was the reason he took a shot at you?"

"Pure cussedness is all I can think of."

"Didn't he hit either of you?"

"He grazed my face; we came down to ask an explanation, and my colored companion was giving him a good pummeling, when you came up and scared him away."

"I take it, stranger, that that contraption over there is one of them infarnal flying machines."

"It is a flying machine, but there's nothing infernal about it."

"Folks hain't no bus'ness to cavort round the country in them."

"I don't see why they haven't; we are not injuring you or any one else."

"Boys," said the speaker, turning to his companions who were standing near and listening to the conversation; "the best thing we can do is to rip the blamed thing to slathers. What do you say?"

"Them's our sentiments," replied one while the three nodded.

"Come on then; it won't take us long to make kindling wood of it."

He took a step forward, and then stopped. Harvey had leveled the gun.

"The first one that lays a hand on my aeroplane must be prepared to have daylight let through him."

It was a staggering threat, but in the trying moment, Harvey Hamilton could not help reflecting that the weapon was not only injured, but unloaded. He would be in a sorry situation should they learn the truth.

The strained situation could not last, and he slowly backed toward the machine, holding the weapon in front, ready to be raised again to a level should it become necessary.

"Four of you are rather too much for me," he said with a grim smile.

"Hooh! One of us could lay you out as easy as rolling off a log."

"I am willing to take you one at a time, but I know that as soon as I get the best of him the rest of you will pitch in and do me up."

It was "Bill" who was talking for the four. He grinned and with a snort replied:

"I'd ax nothing better than one crack at you, but there ain't no show with that loaded gun in your hands; nobody but a coward would use that."

"Then you may consider me a coward, for I am on to your tricks."

By this time Harvey had reached his machine, but the problem remained as to how he could seat himself and start the motor without inviting an attack that must overwhelm him and wreck his property. He stood for a minute undecided, while his enemies, less than a dozen paces away, were on the alert for a chance to seize any advantage that offered.

Suddenly the young aviator stepped into his seat, but, standing upright, faced about and confronted them still with gun in hand. They showed an ugly disposition at the prospect of his eluding them, but seemingly there was no way to prevent it.

"If you would like a closer view," Harvey said, "I have no objection, but you must come one at a time. You may do so first."

He indicated Bill, who hesitated:

"No shenanigan!"

"Nothing of the kind, I promise you."

After a moment's pause, he gingerly approached, but showed he was not wholly free from misgiving.

"What do you think of that big wheel?" asked Harvey.

"Hooh! seems to be made of black walnut," replied the other, laying a hand on one of the propeller blades.

"So it is; have you enough muscle to turn it round?"

"That's dead easy," replied Bill, grasping one of the arms and whirling it about with double the force that was necessary.

CHAPTER XII.
PEACEFUL OVERTURES FAIL.

The revolution of the propeller of course started the engine, with such a terrific outburst of noise that Bill instinctively drew back a pace or two. In an instant the blades were spinning round with tremendous velocity, and the aeroplane began moving over the ground with fast increasing speed.

The sight roused Bill, who dashed forward to intercept it. He had almost reached the machine when it bounded upward and glided beyond his grasp. The delighted Harvey tossed the gun toward him, and in a rage at his slip Bill snatched the weapon from the ground and shouted:

"Stop or I'll shoot!"

His action and movement of the lips told the young aviator the substance of the threat, and with a tantalizing gesture he called back:

"Shoot and be hanged!"

Bill was in a savage mood and brought the gun to his shoulder. He aimed carefully, and with the brief distance between the two could hardly have missed had the weapon been in order; but we recall that the hammers were broken, to say nothing of the lack of a full charge in the barrels. Either would have been sufficient to save the fleeing aviator, who having set the machine going, looked round to watch his enemy.

He saw him suddenly lower the gun and then fling it angrily to the ground. No doubt his chagrin was intensified by the remembrance of the chance he had let pass when the youth was really at his mercy. He shook his fist at Harvey, who was now a hundred feet above the ground and going at moderate speed.

In that hurried scrutiny, however, the aviator made a disquieting discovery. Two of the remaining young men were invisible. Doubtless they had dived into the wood in pursuit of the panic-stricken Bohunkus, who of necessity was left in a most dangerous situation. Harvey had been compelled to desert him for the time, though he was the last person in the world to abandon a friend in trouble. How to save him from the vengeance of the baffled party was a serious question.

"If there were only one chasing him," thought Harvey, "I shouldn't care a fig, for Bunk has already proved himself his master, but he will be helpless against four or even two, and it looks as if he will have three at least to fight."

The problem was a puzzling one. The flight of the colored lad was so sudden that he and Harvey had not been able to exchange a word. A few sentences would have effected an understanding. His friend would have told him to make his way to the nearest town and there wait until he could hunt him out and take him aboard again. Moreover, among Bunk's accomplishments was a remarkable fleetness of foot. He could have continued his flight through the wood into the open country and gained enough advantage to offer Harvey the opportunity of picking him up before his enemies interfered.

But it was useless to speculate, since all this was out of the question. Having ascended some three hundred feet, Harvey began slowly circling around, with just enough speed to hold the elevation. He returned so as to hover directly over the head of Bill, who still stood alone on the edge of the wood closely watching him. Thus the situation remained for several minutes, during which Harvey Hamilton met with one of the narrowest escapes of his life.

Feeling that in one respect the countrymen were the masters, he decided to express to Bill, who was evidently the leader of the quartet his willingness to apologize, pay for the injured gun, and leave a liberal tip for Herb, the only one who had suffered during the singular meeting; and then descend, take Bunk aboard and bid good-bye to the inhospitable country.

The objection to the plan was the probability of treachery on the part of Bill and his companions. All had shown an ugly disposition and so much resentment that it was more than likely they would break the agreement, and at least destroy the aeroplane so utterly as to place it beyond repair.

It was this misgiving that caused Harvey to hesitate. He circled several times—always to the left—gradually descending, and kept watch of the solitary figure below him. Finally, having made his decision, he leaned over the side of the aeroplane and shouted as he slowed down the motor:

"Say, Bill, what's the use of our quarreling?"

Bill did not attempt to answer the conundrum.

"If I do the fair thing, will you call it off?"

"What do you mean by the fair thing?" demanded the surly young man.

"I broke that gun and will pay you for it; I'll give you ten dollars to hand to Herb, though I don't see why he should get anything."

Bill was silent a minute, as if turning the proposition over in his mind. Finally he glared upward and uttered the one query:

"Wal?"

"When I have done that, I shall take my colored friend aboard and have the honor of bidding you good day until we meet again."

This was a clear proposal and could not fail to impress Bill favorably, no matter whether he meant to "tote fair" or not. Bill didn't seem able to think of any objection or to suggest an amendment.

"All right," he shouted back; "I'll do it."

Harvey meant there should be no room for a misunderstanding.

"I am to come down to the ground, hand you ten dollars as a salve—"

"I guess Herb will need some salve for that face of his," grimly interjected Bill.

"And another ten dollars to pay for the damages to the gun. That will make everything right between us and none of you will interfere further."

"I'm agreeable; hurry down."

It was at this juncture that Harvey Hamilton received warning of a frightful peril that in another moment would have caught him inextricably. He had started to volplane to the ground, when an impulse caused him to turn his head sufficiently to glance at the man with whom he had just made his agreement. In that passing glimpse, Harvey saw a hand reach from behind the trunk of a large oak at the back of Bill and exchange guns with him.

It was done in a twinkling, only the arm holding the weapon and the corner of the fellow's face showing for an instant, during which he placed in the grasp of Bill a loaded piece and relieved him of the useless one.

There could be no mistake as to the meaning of the sinister action: Bill intended to play false. He would secure the money promised, and quite likely rob Harvey of all that remained, would wreck the aeroplane and shamefully maltreat both youths. But for this discovery, Harvey would have walked into the lion's den the next moment, but with that coolness which was one of his most striking traits, he began edging away and upward, as if it were a part of his plan of manipulating the descent. If Bill chose to use his gun, he was near enough to make only a single shot necessary, and Harvey's object was to get beyond range, before revealing his purpose.

"What are you doing?" called Bill, handling his weapon threateningly.

"I want to make sure the machinery is working right; it will take only a minute."

Bill was partly satisfied, but had no excuse for objecting.

The circling grew wider, until the right height was attained, when Harvey headed toward the dim range of mountains in the distance, with a speed of at least fifty miles an hour. Only a few seconds were needed to place him far beyond range. Checking his motor for an instant so as to permit his voice to be heard, he called to Bill:

"I don't like the looks of that new gun in your hand; don't expect me before to-morrow or some day next week."

In his impotent rage, Bill brought his weapon to his shoulder, took quick aim and discharged both barrels. It was a foolish thing to do, for not one of the shots carried to the aeroplane, all being dissipated long before they could reach it.

Clever as had been the strategy of Harvey, the grave problem remained as to how he was to extricate Bohunkus Johnson from his dangerous situation. Disappointed in capturing the aviator and his machine, the party were quite sure to turn their rage against the colored youth, unless by his superior fleetness he could elude the whole party.

Harvey's altitude gave him a clear view of the patch of woods, which was perhaps a third of a mile in width and double that length. It was the season of the year when the foliage was at its full, and if Bunk gained a fair start he ought to have no trouble in hiding himself from his enemies; but how were he and his friend to come together again?

"It is as hard to decide as it is to figure out why that man behind the oak with his loaded gun did not keep hidden till I came within reach, and then open on me without giving away his scheme as he did; that would have cooked my goose, though they may have felt doubt of getting hands on the machine if they fired before it touched ground."

Without climbing higher, Harvey circled about the woods, scanning the green depths below for some signal from his comrade. Bill and his companion had passed from sight, so that the five were somewhere in the depths of the forest. The aviator glided along the sky over the tree tops without catching a glimpse of anything to give hope. Then he passed a little way beyond the western end and circled about again. He saw a farm house a mile distant, and unless hope presented itself in some form very soon, he determined to go thither in quest of help against the lawless young men.

What was that which suddenly caught his roving eye? On the margin of the wood something flitted for a moment like a bird hopping from one branch to another. He would have believed it was such, had it not been so near the ground. Whisking his binoculars from his shoulder, he scanned the object. His heart thrilled when he recognized a cap swung by a person standing behind the trunk of a large tree.

"It's Bunk!" exclaimed the delighted youth; "his foes are so near that he daresn't show himself."

Harvey was quick to make up his mind. Shutting off power for a moment he called in his clear, ringing voice:

"Wait where you are, Bunk! I'll be back in a minute or two; don't leave till I give the word and then come a-running."

The cap was waved again and Harvey fancied he saw the corner of the negro's countenance as he peered round the trunk.

The fear of the aviator was that the five men who were sure to be watching his movements, knowing he was trying to save his colored companion, would have their attention drawn to the spot over which the aeroplane was hovering. There was the danger that they had heard his call and would act on the hint, but the risk had to be taken.

Harvey next shifted to the opposite side of the wood, where he dallied back and forth for half an hour, as if trying to fix upon a good landing place. He knew he was under the eyes of the angered countrymen, but was certain he had drawn them to that side of the forest, where they were so far from Bohunkus that it would take considerable time for them to return to his neighborhood.

Suddenly the aeroplane darted off like a swallow, skimming over the trees, at the spot selected.

"Quick, Bunk! Don't lose a second! Jump aboard!"

Out of the wood dashed a young man and ran straight for the machine at headlong speed, but he was not Bohunkus Johnson!

CHAPTER XIII.
SCIENCE WINS.

Clever as was Harvey Hamilton, and skilfully as he had played the game, he was outwitted at last, for the individual who rushed toward him was his enemy Bill, and he carried a loaded gun.

Not only that, but after him hurried one, two, three, four others, ready to back up their leader. One of them carried a deadly weapon. Bohunkus Johnson was nowhere in sight.

No wonder the young aviator was dumfounded for the moment. He was still seated, with his hands grasping the levers, but he was too wise to try to flee, with that gun commanding him and the holder of it in the mood to use it. In a twinkling, the grinning Bill was at his side and laid his free hand upon one of the propeller blades.

"Shall I start the thing humming agin?" he asked with grim irony.

Harvey's wits flashed back to him.

"Wait till I do my part," he replied, as if the slightest misunderstanding had not come between them.

As he spoke, he stepped on the ground and drew out his pocket book, while the five stood expectantly around, all not understanding what the action meant.

"I was so afraid we might have some accident with that gun," he remarked, observing the damaged weapon in the hands of one of the party; "that I broke the hammers; you can get them fixed at a gunsmith's for a dollar, so I guess that will about make it right."

With which he handed a ten-dollar bill to Bill, who crumpled it up and shoved it into his pocket, without a word of acknowledgment.

The situation was delicate to the last degree. A few feet away stood Herb, whose homely face spoke eloquently of the scrimmage through which he had passed. One eye was closed, the upper lip was swollen to twice its usual size, and the cheeks were bruised, to say nothing of the rent shirt, with more than one crimson stain showing upon it. To offer to settle the matter by handing the sufferer money was like adding insult to injury, though the majority of mankind have little trouble in swallowing offenses of that nature.

No one could have met the point more tactfully.

"Herb," said Harvey, stepping toward him; "you and my colored man had a run-in and the last I saw of him he was going for life."

"You bet he was!" said the other; "it's blamed lucky for him he run so fast I couldn't ketch him; if I'd done so there would have been a dead nigger in these parts."

Harvey hid the pleasure that this reply gave him. Bunk had escaped from his foe and was safe somewhere.

"He got me foul," Herb added, feeling that some explanation was due his fellows who had seen him in his humiliating situation; "but I throwed him off and then he took to his heels."

Herb added several sulphurous exclamations which it isn't necessary to place on record.

"I saw him running, but I notice that he managed to injure your clothes and it is no more than right that the damage should be taken out of his wages. Will this make it square?"

When Herb saw the size of the bill handed to him his little gray eyes— or rather one of them—sparkled with greed. But the three who had not been thus remembered were angered.

"Say, boss, you seem to have a purty good wad there; 'spose you hand out a few more of the long green."

This suggestive remark was made by the scowling scamp who answered to the name of Sam. As if there should be no doubt of his meaning, Bill took it upon himself to add:

"That's right; you don't need any money when you've got that sky wagon to tote you about. So fork over."

Harvey's face flushed, but holding his anger under control, he said to Bill:

"The agreement between us was that if I handed this money to you, my colored friend was to rejoin me and neither he nor I nor the machine be molested."

"How can the moke jine you when he's run off?" asked Herb.

"We'll waive that point, but you are not to injure my machine nor expect any more money from me."

"Do you mean to say you won't give it?" demanded Bill truculently.

"I'll die first; I didn't know you were a gang of cowards as well as scoundrels."

"Who're you calling a coward?" growled Bill, his sunburned face flushing an angrier red.

"Every one of you! Five against one; you wouldn't dare attack me singly."

"I wouldn't, hooh? Boys," added the bully, addressing his companions, "this lily is my game. You don't have any put here. Understand?"

They sourly nodded, though little or no reliance could be placed on any promise they might make.

"Will you agree to fight me alone?" asked Harvey.

"Of course; that suits me down to the ground."

"And the rest are not to mix in, no matter what happens?"

"Hain't I told you that? What ails you?"

"That suits me," replied Harvey, who coolly took off his coat and flung it across the footrest of the aeroplane. If anything like fair play was shown him, he had no fear of the result, for though his antagonist was taller and possibly stronger, he knew nothing of the science of boxing. Having doffed his outer garment, Harvey proceeded in the same deliberate fashion to roll up his sleeves. Then he poised his right fist a few inches in front of his chest and diagonally across it, with the left extended toward his antagonist. The left foot was advanced so that the weight of his body rested on the right leg, so balanced that he could leap forward or backward as might suddenly become necessary. His handsome face was a shade paler, and he compressed his lips as he said in a quiet even voice:

"I'm ready!"

The prospect of a fight between two men or even boys is always sure to interest the spectators no matter who they may be. Every one of the five men was in a state of delighted expectation, for not an individual felt the faintest doubt that the dandified youth was about to undergo the beating of his life. The four were ready to promise they would remain neutral, for they could not believe a possibility existed of their champion needing help.

As for Bill himself, he chuckled, for he dearly loved a fight and he felt venomous toward this intruder, because he seemed to be rich and had lately played a humiliating trick upon him. He handed his gun to Dick, but did not remove his coat, because he did not happen to be wearing any. He made a motion with each hand in turn, as if to shove the bands of his shirt toward the elbow, but he merely tightened them. He did indulge, however, in a little act that is generally peculiar to a countryman. He spat on his horny palms and rubbed them together.

Harvey saw from the first that though Bill might be a powerful man, he lacked even a rudimentary knowledge of boxing. He held his fists in front, but they were well down, separated by a wide space, and when he drew near enough to deliver a blow, his feet were side by side. While Harvey Hamilton's pose was an ideal one, that of Bill was the opposite.

In contests of this nature, the sympathies of the reader are naturally with the "gentleman," and the story teller generally arranges that he shall be the victor, though in real life it is not likely to happen that way. Had the elder undergone the training of the younger, he assuredly would have beaten him to a "frazzle," but it was that one thing lacking which proved the undoing of Bill.

His awkward advance upon the youth gave the latter the opening he was waiting for, and coolly, promptly and fiercely he seized the advantage. Bill lunged out terrifically, but the blow was a round one and being cleverly parried, swished in front of Harvey's face. In the same instant his opponent made a single bound forward, so as to throw the weight of his body into the straight, lightning-like thrust of the left fist, which crashed against Bill's receding chin with the force of a mule's kick. He went over on his back, completely knocked out and with no more sense than a log of wood. It may be said that the fight was ended before it fairly began.

Harvey knew some seconds must pass before Bill would be able to climb to his feet. He shifted front in a flash and said:

"I'm waiting for the next."

He still held his arms in position and danced deftly about as if impatient over the slight delay in their attack. But their hesitation was due more to bewilderment than fear, though the sight of the motionless form stretched on the ground told its own story.

It would be thought that the courage shown by the young pugilist would have appealed to the manhood of the others, but, sad to say, they had no manhood to which appeal could be made. The one known as Dick shouted:

"Are we going to stand that, boys? Didn't you see him hit Bill? He hit him foul! Let's lay him out!"

Harvey braved himself for the shameless attack, determined to make their victory cost them dear. He knew that more than one would suffer, but a pang shot through him when Dick called out:

"Let's smash that old thing to flinders first and then serve him the same way."

"That's the idee!" answered Sam; "we'll make one job of it!"

And they charged together to carry out their cowardly threat.

CHAPTER XIV.
MILO MORGAN SAVES THE DAY.

As straight downward as if fired from the zenith, a tiny missile shot through the air so swiftly that no one saw it. It struck the ground directly in front of the four men and burst with a deafening report. In the same second, another followed the first, landing just behind the group with the same terrifying explosion. All saw the flash, the smoke and the flying particles.

Then a third and fourth followed with similar results. Succeeding the fire and crash a voice rang out:

"Run for your lives! Take to the woods or you are dead men!"

The command, which sounded as if it came from heaven, acted like an electric shock upon the four young men, who with gasps of dismay dived in among the trees with such headlong panic that two dropped their hats, and the others stumbled, crawling forward and scrambling to their feet as best they could.

The bewildered Harvey might have done the same, for it seemed the only way of escaping a frightful death, had he not fancied there was a familiar note in the deep bass voice. When he looked aloft, the strange occurrence was explained. Balanced directly overhead and not more than a hundred feet high, floated a monoplane. A slim man more than six feet tall and clothed in a long flapping duster was standing erect with a small, oblong object in his hand to which he had just applied a match. He let it hiss for a moment, and then tossed it away so that it fell only a few feet from where Harvey stood.

"Don't be scared," he called; "I'm just practicing how to drop a bomb on the deck of a vessel; these things make a loud noise but nothing more."

As the delighted youth stared upward, he saw painted in glaring letters on the under side of the single plane the words:

"THE DRAGON OF THE SKIES."

"Aren't you coming down to call?" asked Harvey. "No one could be so welcome as you."

"So I judged from the way things looked; I have been up here some time watching matters. You keeled over that brute beautifully."

"He is showing signs of revival."

"Stand a little out of the way and watch me help revive him."

Harvey, relieved beyond expression by the happy turn of affairs, sprang several paces aside and watched his friend aloft. He was still standing erect, balanced so perfectly in the calm that he did not have to steady himself. The missiles which he had flung to the earth were simply giant firecrackers, some six inches long and more than an inch in diameter. He knew when he lighted the powder-soaked string which served as a fuse how many seconds it would require to reach the powder within. It has been shown how accurate he was in his calculations.

Harvey saw the flicker of the smoking match as it was touched to the short dangling twist of fuse attached to the cracker which he held in his left hand beside his waist, while with one eye closed he squinted along the red tube as if aiming a gun. Then he parted his thumb and forefinger and the cracker tumbled downward end over end, and either through extraordinary skill or by good luck dropped upon the chest of Bill and burst with terrific force and deafening noise.

It certainly "revived" the man, for with a howl he leaped to his feet and plunged in among the trees in the wildest panic conceivable. A fifty-pound bombshell would have caused more damage but could not have created greater terror.

Harvey in the reaction of his spirits leaned against his biplane to keep from falling through excessive mirth. He had never seen anything so funny in his life. In the midst of his merriment, Professor Milo Morgan called down:

"I must be off; good-bye; better not bother with such folks as these."

"But, Professor, won't you make me a call?"

"Haven't time; other matters are awaiting me."

"Can you tell me anything about Bohunkus?"

"He's round on the other side of the wood, waiting for you."

As he spoke, the elongated aviator extended one arm, so that no doubt was left of the direction meant. Then he resumed his seat, and the Dragon of the Skies darted into space like an eagle diving from his mountain perch.

Harvey noticed again that swiftly as the man was speeding, his monoplane seemed to emit no noise whatever. It was certainly a remarkable muffler that enabled him to do this, and it explained why none of the party below had any inkling of the crank's proximity until he made it known in the startling manner described. Moreover his uplifter held him sustained without motion, as we sometimes see a bird hovering over the ocean and preparing to dart downward for its prey.

"He has made enough inventions already to give him riches beyond estimate, but the fact seems to be the last to enter his head."

But Harvey could not forget his dusky comrade. Professor Morgan had told where he could be found, provided he had not gone elsewhere in the meantime. The five young men with whom the couple had had their affray were still capable of making trouble. It was possible that when they found none was harmed, they would return to look into matters. The minutes were too valuable to be wasted.

Although the aeroplane had been exposed to danger it had suffered no injury. Instead of procuring a brake, in the form of a prop from the nearby wood, with which to hold the machine until momentum was gathered, the young aviator whirled the propeller about, stepped into his seat and grasped the control. The motor started at once and sent out its deafening racket. The little rubber-tired wheels began slowly turning and sped swiftly across the open space. Harvey waited until he was going very fast, when he drew back the handle and in the same instant felt he was traveling on nothing. Upward and outward he shot to a height of three hundred feet, when he circled about and came back over the wood, beyond which he glided to the other side.

It was there he ought to find Bohunkus. Slowing his progress as much as he could and still remain aloft, he scanned the earth in quest of the colored youth. There was the stretch of woodland, meadow and sparsely cultivated ground, with the small dwelling in the distance, the landscape being crossed by a winding creek which skirted the forest and lost itself far to the eastward.

But Bohunkus Johnson was nowhere to be seen.

"Likely enough he has started off on a run again with nobody chasing him and may not look behind until he has gone several miles. It would serve him right if I left him to get home the best he can. He has enough money to pay his way and—."

Harvey's eye rested on a large maple lying on the edge of the wood. It had fallen recently, for the foliage of the abundant limbs was still green. The trunk, which must have been two feet in diameter at the base, showed no branches for several yards, but was held a little above the ground by the sturdy and bent limbs upon which the greater weight was resting.

There was no particular reason why this object should interest Harvey, but it did, and he scrutinized it closely, as he slowly sailed past. Something moved, but so vaguely that he could not identify it. The object appeared to be under the log in the open space between it and the ground upon which it was supported. The distance was so trifling that Harvey did not call his binoculars into use.

The top of a person's head, without a cap or covering except a mass of black wool, and a pair of staring eyes, showed over the top of the log. Their owner was watching the biplane, as if uncertain of its identity. Had the individual remained stationary, he would have come into clear view, as Harvey glided beyond him, but before that could take place, he ducked under the maple, whisked beneath, and raising his head, again peered over the trunk from the other side. He did not speak, but evidently was mystified and undecided what to do.

The amused Harvey curved about and then volplaned to the ground within fifty paces of the fallen tree. As he did so, he saw Bohunkus standing erect and grinning at him. He had donned his cap and was delighted.

"Did I scare yo'?" he asked, going forward to meet his friend.

"Scare me? How could you do that?"

"I knowed it was yo' all de time; I thought I'd have a little fun wid yo'."

"What were you doing behind that log, Bunk?"

"Nuffin; I felt sorter tired and laid down to rest till yo' come along; I was getting out ob patience wid yo'; what made yo' so late?"

"I have been looking for you; those were queer performances on your part."

"What oblusions am yo' obluding to, Harv?"

"You gave that fellow the best thumping he ever had, and then jumped up and ran off like a big coward."

"Didn't run away from nobody; it was dem 'leben fellers wid dere loaded guns dat was a chasing me like all creation; wouldn't yo' run yo'self?"

"Certainly, if I had been attacked by such a force, but I stayed behind and entertained the other four and there was only the one that troubled you. What became of that fellow who tried so hard to overtake you?"

"He's dead," was the solemn answer of Bunk.

"What killed him?"

"Me," was the unblushing response; "I kept running till I got him away from de oder nine, so dey couldn't help him; den I whirled about and lammed him so hard dat it was de last ob him; he'll neber insult any 'spectable colored gemman agin."

"Well, Bunk, I am afraid you will have to do your job over, for I saw him only a little while ago. He may be near at hand this minute."

And Harvey glanced around as if alarmed by the probability of such a thing.

"Being dat am de way things stand, hadn't we better emigrate, Harv?"

CHAPTER XV.
UNCLE TOMMY.

Like a sensible young man, Harvey Hamilton had made a study of his itinerary before leaving home. Allowing himself a margin of several days, he expected to rejoin his friends at the end of a fortnight. If all went well he would do so earlier, while there was always the possibility that he might be absent still longer.

He knew that the little town nestling several miles to the left was Darmore. It was at the base of a spur of the Alleghanies toward which he had been working his way from the first. His wish was to pass beyond the thickly settled districts. Nothing palls sooner upon an aviator than the endless succession of towns, villages, cultivated sections and monotonous scenery. While there must be a certain sameness in the expanses of forest there was always the chance of adventure which a normal youngster craves as he does his meals when hungry.

Harvey had meditated going to Darmore to renew his supply of fuel, but recalled that after passing the mountain ridge, another and larger town lay some miles away in the broad forest valley. He had enough gasoline to carry him thither and he decided to make the trip. He followed his general rule of not rising far above the altitude necessary to clear the tallest trees and elevations. Thus, viewed far from the rear, the aeroplane suggested that it was climbing the mountain side by resting upon and sailing over the billowy sea of foliage.

The summit proper was no more than two or three hundred yards in height, and having cleared it the young aviator mounted higher than before in order to secure a comprehensive view of the surrounding country and learn how correct his impressions were.

He was vastly pleased. Almost in a direct line and not far away lay Chesterton, a town of several thousand population and in the midst of a thriving section of the country. He traced the winding highways, the scattered farm houses, the broad, cultivated fields, the signs of busy life everywhere, and the enormous wealth of forest which continued up the farther slope, crowned the top of the ridge and stretched down the incline beyond.

The noisy motor in the sky and the queer looking object which seemed to be advancing sideways and at a rapid pace, drew attention wherever it was seen. Farmers riding over the dusty roads stopped their teams and stared aloft until they got kinks in their necks; men and women climbed to the roofs of their houses, as if the slight decrease of distance would help them, and breathlessly studied the strange sight, some of the spectators with the aid of spy-glasses; groups gathered on lawns, porches and in front of their homes; every window of a passenger train, to say nothing of the platforms, was wedged with curious observers, while several white puffs which shot upward from the steam whistle showed that the engineer was sending out a salutation to the aerial wanderer who could not hear it. Everybody had read of aeroplanes and seen pictures of them, but this was the first time the real thing had sailed into their sea of vision and no picture can stir like the actuality itself.

Two men, one of them carrying a gun, were walking over the high road, a little way to the right, and probably two hundred yards from the aeroplane. They had stopped and were surveying the strange object overhead. One of them abruptly raised his weapon and the little faint blue puff showed he had used the machine as his target. Instead of a shotgun the fellow fired a rifle. It was impossible of course to hear the report, but the sudden appearance of a small white spot on the framework of the upper wing, showed where the bullet had nipped off a splinter. Strange that so many people cannot observe a curious object without yearning to shoot it.

Harvey looked around at Bohunkus, and by a nod and the expression of his face asked whether he wished to be set down that he might properly chastise the scamp. The colored youth shook his head. He had gone through enough in that line to satisfy him. Harvey shied off and speedily passed beyond range. The fellow did not try a second shot.

Thus far the weather had been ideal, but a disagreeable change threatened. The sun was hidden by clouds, which increased in density and number, and the air became so chilly that both shivered. Harvey headed for Chesterton, for it was evident that soon all pleasure in aerial sailing would be ended for the time.

The approach of the aeroplane roused the usual excitement in the little country town, and when Harvey descended in an open space near the collection of houses, half a hundred people rushed thither to greet and give him whatever help he needed. He aimed to make a graceful landing so as properly to impress the spectators, but he got another reminder of the astonishing sensitiveness of the aeroplane, which must be handled far differently from an automobile. He was not quick enough in shifting the lever and hit the ground with so violent a bump that Bohunkus, who was not expecting anything of the kind, was thrown headlong from his perch and landed in a sitting posture with so loud a grunt that the onlookers laughed.

"What's de matter wid yo'?" he asked angrily; "dat's de right way to come down in an airyplane. Hab yo' any 'bjections?"

"It's the way you land," replied one of the men, "because you don't know any better."

Bohunkus would have been glad to make a scathing retort, but was unable to think of one. So he said in the way of reproof to his companion:

"De next time yo's gwine to try to knock a hole fru de airth, let me know so I can jump."

"It will do you as much good to jump afterward as before. It looks to me as if a storm is coming, Bunk, and we must get the machine under shelter."

The pleasant feature about the situation was that the crowd which had gathered and continued to gather was a friendly one. No one spoke an ill-natured word and all were eager to help in every way possible.

When Harvey stood on the ground, facing the group, he asked:

"Are we going to have a rain?"

"He's the man that'll tell you all about the weather for a week to come and hit it every time."

The one who spoke pointed to an old farmer, without coat or waistcoat, with a ragged straw hat, chin whiskers and bent shoulders, who was chewing tobacco after the manner of a cow masticating her cud.

"How is it, Uncle Tommy?" asked the man who had just spoken.

The old fellow, still chewing, looked up at the sky and then around the heavens, squinting one eye as he carefully studied the signs.

"It'll rain like all creation inside of a couple of hours; then it'll hold up a little while and bime by start in agin and drizzle all night."

"How about to-morrow?" asked Harvey.

"It'll be bright and clear, but a little cooler than to-day."

"Tell the young gentleman how the rest of the week will be," insisted his neighbor.

"The next three days will be clear and rayther warmish; I won't say anything beyond that this afternoon, but if ye wanter know, I'll obleege ye to-morrer when I've had a snifter and my breakfast."

"I am much obliged; you have told me what I wanted to know. I shall need shelter for this aeroplane; can any of you gentlemen help me?"

There was less difficulty than Harvey anticipated. Chesterton had a single large hotel or tavern as the townspeople called it, with the usual rows of sheds for the convenience of countrymen when they drove in from the neighborhood. With the help of several bystanders the machine was shoved over the road and through the alley—where much care was necessary to save the wings from injury—to the sheds at the rear. There, after some delicate maneuvering, the machine was worked into the shelter at the corner, where a fair hangar was secured.

"Here we stay till the weather clears," said Harvey to Bunk, as they strolled into the hotel to get their dinner, for which each had a keen appetite.

Where all showed so hospitable a disposition, Harvey felt little fear of any harm to the aeroplane, though Bohunkus strolled out once or twice to make sure everything was right. After the meal the young aviator seated himself in the utility room, as it may be called. This was connected by a door that was always open with the bar, and was intended for the convenience of those who wished something a little less public. It was provided with several chairs, a round table standing in the middle of the apartment, and had a sanded floor and a few cheap sporting prints on the walls. A half dozen men were seated around, most of them with feet elevated on other chairs or the window sills, while they gossiped of the affairs of the neighborhood. They showed little interest in Harvey and Bunk. The former obtained pen, paper and ink from the landlord and spent a part of the afternoon in writing to his parents and to brother Dick in the Adirondacks. He named a town in advance which he expected to reach at the end of a week, as the proper one to which to address their replies. This duty attended to, Harvey looked at Bunk, whose cap had fallen on the floor as he leaned back in his chair and slept. There was no prejudice so far as yet shown against his race in that section and he was not annoyed by any one.

Recalling the words of the old weather prophet, Harvey went out on the long covered porch in front of the hotel. The two hours had passed and the rain was coming down in torrents. Then, just as the venerable farmer had said would be the case, it slackened, with the promise of renewal before nightfall.

"Some of those old fellows can beat the government every time," reflected Harvey; "I shall believe Uncle Tommy until I see the proof of his mistake. Well, I declare!"

It happened at that moment that Harvey Hamilton was the only person on the porch, where several wooden chairs awaited occupants. Here and there a man or woman could be seen hurrying along the sloppy street, all eager to reach home or shelter. The youth's exclamation was caused by sight of an unusually tall man, in a long, flapping linen duster, striding forward on the same side as the tavern, so that he passed within a dozen paces of where the astonished youth stared wonderingly at him, for, without his distinctive attire, the long grizzled beard and glowing black eyes identified him at once.

"How are you, Professor?" called Harvey; "I'm mighty glad to see you again."

The individual upon being hailed looked at the young man as if he had never seen him before, and then, without the slightest sign of recognition, stalked up the street and out of sight.

CHAPTER XVI.
A MYSTERIOUS COMMUNICATION.

Harvey Hamilton stood speechless. When he spoke to Professor Morgan, they were no more than a rod apart, with only the broad open space in front of the hotel between them. Upon hearing himself addressed, the man had looked straight into the face of the lad and then, as already said, passed on without the faintest sign of recognition.

A more direct snub cannot be imagined, and yet it was not in the nature of a snub. Nothing had occurred that could justify so marked a slight. The humiliation which Harvey felt for a few seconds quickly passed away.

"He must have been too absorbed in reverie to see me, and yet that can't be possible, for he showed that he heard me call him by his title."

By and by the young aviator reached the only conclusion that seemed reasonable.

"He is a crank in every sense of the word; he is as crazy as a June bug; he was friendly enough last night and this forenoon, and now he is in a different mood. Well, I shall always feel grateful for the good turn he did me. If we meet again, he may be in a more genial frame of mind; at least I hope so."

The downpour was increasing and the air had become so chilly that Harvey passed inside to the sitting-room. The same number of men were present as before, smoking, chewing and gossiping. He glanced into their countenances, as he moved his chair beside the sleeping Bohunkus Johnson, prepared to pass the dismal hours as best he could without finding any reading matter in the form of books or newspapers. He had registered before dinner and engaged a room for himself and another for his companion. His letters were given to the landlord, who promised to send them to the post office in time for the afternoon's mail.

Somehow or other, there was one man among the group in whom Harvey felt a slight interest, though he attributed the fact to the lack of anything else to engage his mind. This individual was standing at the desk, when Harvey came from the outside, studying the dog-eared register, as if he too was guided by some idle impulse. He glanced at the newcomer and followed him into the larger room, where he lighted a cigar and took a seat against the other wall.

He was of slight frame, in middle life, dressed in a gray business suit, with clean shaven face, a thin sharp nose, good teeth and keen blue eyes. He was alert of manner, and might well have been a drummer held in town for a brief while against his will. When Harvey glanced at him again he quickly averted his eyes. Apparently he did not wish to be detected in the act and he came within a hair of succeeding in his attempt. He gazed in an absent way through the door leading to the bar-room and smoked his cigar like a man who thoroughly enjoyed the weed.

Being in an idle mood, Harvey twisted the corner of his handkerchief into a tight spiral, making the end quite stiff and pointed, and, leaning forward, began drawing it back and forth against the base of the sleeping Bohunkus Johnson's nose. Immediately every other person in the room began watching the proceedings.

For a little while the negro slept on undisturbed. Then he suddenly crinkled his broad, flat nose and flipped his hand at the fly or mosquito that was supposed to be tickling him. The spectators grinned, and Harvey waited till Bunk was slumbering as heavily as before. Then he resumed his role of Tantalus. This time he tickled so energetically that Bunk struck impatiently at his tormentor and banged the top of the chair a vigorous blow—so vigorous indeed that several of the men snickered and the dusky youth opened his eyes and raised his head, as wide awake as ever in his life.

"Think yo's smart, doan' yo'?" he growled, donning the cap that had fallen to the floor and shaking himself together.

"The next thing, Bunk, you'll fall asleep in the biplane and tumble out head first."

"I doan' see dat it'll make any difference to yo' if I do," replied the other, nettled by the general laughter more than by the manner of his awaking.

"It won't, but it will to you. If you want to sleep all the time go to your room."

Bohunkus mumbled something, shifted his position, sank down in his chair until he seemed to be sitting on the upper part of his spine, and in a few minutes was nodding again. Harvey molested him no further, but looking up discovered by a furtive glance that the thin young man in gray had been studying him for an indefinite time, though quick to shift his gaze as before.

Harvey drew his note-book from his pocket, and, bringing his chair to the table, began making sketches with his pencil, wholly from imagination. The stranger, a little while later, drew up his seat opposite and busied himself in the same way. Thus the situation remained for perhaps ten minutes.

Suddenly a pellet of paper the size of a dime was flipped across the brief space and fell upon the page that was covered with Harvey's tracings. He knew it came from the man on the other side of the table, and he understood it was meant to be secret. It was an extraordinary way by which to communicate with him, when it would have been easy to speak one or two words in so guarded tones that they could not be overheard. But the man must have had his reasons, which would appear later.

With that quickness of resource that has been shown to be a marked trait of Harvey Hamilton, he did a bright thing. Without betraying any haste or interest, he picked up the tiny wad and slipped it into his waistcoat pocket. He did not even look at the stranger, but nodded his head, keeping his eyes on his note-book. A minute later the man rose from his chair and sauntered into the bar-room, turning off to one side so as to be out of sight of the youth had he looked for him while still in his seat, which he did not.

It was with curious emotions that Harvey saw he was called upon to play a peculiar role. He had been given a written communication in such a manner as to make it certain the sender wished no other person to know what had taken place. The youth must read the message, but do so secretly. To untwist the bit and examine it while in the sitting-room would betray everything. Only one course remained.

It was not yet dark, for it will be remembered it was summer time, but stepping to the bar, behind which the landlord was standing serving a customer, Harvey asked for the key to his room. It was handed to him from a nail and he was directed to ascend the stairs to the upper hall, along which he was to walk until he saw the number "34" on the door.

As Harvey started to follow directions, he glanced about the bar-room, in which there were six or eight persons, but the author of the mysterious message was not among them. He was standing on the porch outside, and looked for an instant through the window at Harvey, but no sign or signal was exchanged between them.

Not until he had entered his room and locked the door did Harvey unroll the paper pellet, and, standing by the window where the light was good, read the following words:

"I shall knock at your door at nine o'clock this evening. Keep your colored servant out of the way. I have something important to say to you. When we meet outside of your room neither must show that he has ever met the other. Don't fail me.

S. P."

After the perplexity caused by these curious sentences, Harvey Hamilton's feeling was that of amusement.

"I have come to Chesterton in my aeroplane, and dived head first into one of the most tremendous mysteries that ever was. Bunk and I set out to find adventure and it looks as if we had struck it rich. But what the mischief can it all mean?"

Try as hard as he might, he could not take the matter as seriously as it seemed to him he ought to do. The time was well on in the twentieth century, he was in one of the most civilized sections of the Union, and things as a rule were conducted in accordance with law. Surely "S. P." was not hinting at murder, or burglary, or incendiarism, or any other heinous crime.

"What is he driving at and who is he?"

Harvey Hamilton would not have been a bright, high-spirited youth of seventeen years had he not been stirred by the curious communication that had been delivered so oddly to him. He speculated and theorized, and the more he did so the more he was puzzled.

"Some folks like to be mysterious," he said, "and the less cause they have for being so the more secret they are. Why didn't 'S. P.', whoever he is, drop me a word, which he could have done without it being noticed by any one else?

"It must have been there was another person in the room that he was afraid would become suspicious, but I have no idea who he was. It is odd that this fellow is the only one who interested me.

"What can his business be with me? I was never in this part of the world before and haven't had anything to do with the people here, nor anywhere in the neighborhood, except those young men this forenoon. It can't have any relation to them, for they have not had time to reach Chesterton since our run-in."

"How about Professor Morgan?" Harvey asked himself with a start. "I know he is in town and didn't show any pleasure when I recognized him. Can it be that he and 'S. P.' have anything between them in which I am concerned?"

He sat for a long time turning over the perplexing subject in his mind, with the only result of becoming more befogged.

"Pshaw! what's the use?" he exclaimed impatiently, as he came to his feet and donned his cap; "it is nearly night and I have to wait but a few hours, when he will make everything clear. So here goes."

He locked his door behind him and started down the long hall. At the head of the stairs, whom should he meet but the alert looking man in gray? Harvey was about to suggest that they return to his room together and have their conference, but the other did not seem to see him; and recalling the warning, the youth passed down the steps as if he had encountered an utter stranger. The latter did not show up at the supper table and Harvey was relieved, for it would have been some embarrassment to him. It may have been the man's knowledge of this fact that caused him to keep out of the way.

Time passed slowly. When Harvey looked at his watch and saw that it lacked fifteen minutes of the time appointed, he started for his room. Bohunkus had already gone up stairs. When he bade his friend good night, he said to him:

"I need sleep, Bunk, so stay in your room till I call you in the morning."

"All right; I hain't no 'bjection; I sha'n't get up till yo' bang on my door."

CHAPTER XVII.
CALLED TO THE RESCUE.

Harvey Hamilton struck a match, after he had unlocked the door of his room and stepped inside. He lighted the gas and seated himself beside the stand in front of the mirror, to wait the brief interval. He continually glanced at his watch and twice held it to his ear to make sure it had not stopped. At three minutes to nine, he slipped it into his pocket, leaned back and listened.

"I shall soon hear his footstep," was his thought; "everything is so still that if he comes in his stocking feet it will be perceptible on the bare floor——"

But, though the listening youth had not caught the slightest noise, he now heard a gentle tap, tap. He stepped hastily across the room and drew the door open. The gas light in the apartment showed the man in gray wrapped in the fainter illumination of the hall around and behind him. He did not speak until he had stepped inside. Then in the lowest and softest of voices he said:

"If you don't mind," gently turning the key in the closed door, and stepping forward so as to be as far as possible from the threshold. As if still uneasy, he glanced under the bed as his head came on a level with the post. Then he rose and peeped into the closet, where nothing hung but the outer coat of the rightful occupant.

"You will excuse me, Harvey, but I must make sure we are alone," said the man apologetically.

The host felt a touch of surprise at being addressed by his given name, but smiled as he also seated himself, with only the width of the little stand in the middle of the room between them.

"You need have no misgivings, sir; we are as much alone as if we were a mile high in my aeroplane."

Asking permission, the guest lighted a cigar and hitched as near as he could to the young man.

"You were surprised to receive that note from me?"

"My surprise was due as much to the style of delivery as to its contents. Why didn't you use your tongue instead of your pencil?"

"Two men in the room were watching me."

"Didn't they see you flip the paper?"

"No; without looking directly at them I knew when their heads were turned and they were occupied with that dispute in the bar-room. Then it was that the bit of paper which I was holding and awaiting my chance, dropped on the page of your note-book. Had I spoken, they would have heard me, though they might not have understood the words, but no sound was made by the tiny missive."

"It would have been natural for me to betray you by my surprise, and to open the fragment and read it at the time their attention came back to the room in which we were all sitting."

"I knew you were not that kind of a young man."

The compliment did not wholly please Harvey.

"How could you know that? What means had you of learning anything about me? I noticed that you know my first name."

"The hotel register told me that you are Harvey Hamilton, from Mootsport, New Jersey; a little study of you when you did not suspect what I was doing imparted the rest. We detectives become skilful in reading character."

"So you are a detective?" said Harvey in surprise, such a thought never having come to him until this announcement was made.

"That is my profession, but you are the only person in Chesterton who suspects anything of the kind."

"You mean you believe so, but, brilliant as are detectives—that is some of them—they occasionally make mistakes."

"They would not be human if they did not."

"But some blunder less than others. You signed your note with your initials, 'S. P.' I have some curiosity to know what they stand for."

"The hotel register would have told you."

"But I had not enough interest to look; I feel different now."

"You may call me Simmons Pendar."

"Knowing at the same time that it is not your real name."

"But will serve as well as any other."

"I am sure I have no objection; well, Mr. Simmons Pendar, I am in my room to keep the appointment you requested. I await your pleasure."

It may be said that the professional detective, as he announced himself, was somewhat surprised by his reception. He supposed that his host—inasmuch as he was only a boy—would be markedly impressed when he learned the profession of his caller, but he seemed almost indifferent. Pendar was pleased, for it helped to confirm the opinion he had formed of the mental acuteness of the lad.

"I have no intention of assuming the mysterious, Harvey, as some people are fond of doing. Since I have told you I am a detective, you naturally wonder what possible business I can have with you."

"You guessed right the first time."

"I assume that you are willing to aid me in the cause of justice."

"You have no right to assume that, for our ideas of justice, as you term it, may differ."

The visitor laughed, but without the least noise.

"Well said! But I am sure we shall agree in this business."

"That remains to be seen." And Harvey continued his attitude of close attention. Detective Pendar came to the point with a rush:

"Some weeks ago Grace Hastings, the five-year-old daughter of the wealthy Mr. and Mrs. Horace Hastings, of Philadelphia, was stolen by members of the Italian Black Hand, who hold her for a heavy ransom. Perhaps you read the account?"

"I did," replied Harvey, compressing his lips as his eyes flashed; "I was never so angered in my life. This kidnapping business has become so common during the last few years that I should like to help in burning some of the Mafia and Black Hand devils at the stake. There's more excuse for such punishment than for burning those black imps in the South."

The youth was so wrought up that he bounded to his feet and paced rapidly up and down the room. His caller coolly watched him and remained silent. The result of his revelation was what he wished it to be.

The leaven was working. When Harvey became calmer, he resumed his seat, but his white face betrayed his tense emotion.

"Would you like to help to rescue the little girl and bring the scoundrels to justice?"

"I would give anything in the world for the chance."

"You have it!"

"What do you mean?" demanded Harvey, bounding to his feet again.

"Just what I said; pull yourself together and listen."

"Don't keep me waiting."

"You are making an excursion through the air with your aeroplane; this fact gives you an advantage which may prove a deciding one. I need not dwell on the grief of the parents of the little one, which is worse than death itself could cause. They will give any amount of money to recover their only child from the grip of those wretches. They have employed many detectives in searching for her; I have been doing nothing else for six weeks."

"Why don't they pay the ransom? That has been done in other cases, with the result of recovering the stolen one."

"The father wished to pay the demand as soon as it came to him, but somebody or something has convinced him that it will prove only the first of other demands still more exorbitant, with the recovery of the child much in doubt."

"Has no clue been obtained as to the whereabouts of the little girl?"

"There's been no end of clues, but they lead nowhere. The mother in her frantic grief insists that her husband shall pay the price without more delay, and I believe he will not hold out much longer, satisfied that it is the only hope left to him."

"But how can I give any help with my aeroplane?"

"I have reason to think the gang has its headquarters not many miles from this place."

Harvey looked his astonishment.

"If that is true, what prevents you from running them down?"

"An almost insurmountable difficulty faces me. I am the only searcher who holds this theory, as I am the only one who has reason for it. But it is diamond cut diamond. These miscreants are alert, shrewd and cunning to the last degree. They have their watchers out, and upon the first sign of danger they will signal the others, who will make a lightning change of base, taking the child with them."

"Have you any idea of the spot where they are?"

"Only that it is several miles away, in the depth of the forest which covers so large an extent of this mountainous country."

"Then why in heaven's name don't you and a posse rush them?" asked Harvey, impatient with what seemed the dilatoriness of the officer.

"No one man nor a dozen men could find their way over the faint trails in time to surprise the gang. They keep lookouts on duty day and night. There isn't a stranger who comes to Chesterton that is not watched. Two of their men are in the hotel this minute; they have had you and even your stupid colored youth under scrutiny."

"Have they any suspicion of me?" asked Harvey with a grim smile.

"No; for you are too young and your actions are too open."

"How about yourself?"

"I am hopeful that they are in the dark regarding me, though I am not positive; I am playing the role of a drummer for a hardware firm in New York. I have taken quite a number of orders, and all the time have been on the watch for a chance to go upon an exploring expedition through the surrounding wilderness. You understand the delicacy of my situation. A single attempt in that line, even if immediately abandoned, will give me away and end all possibility of my accomplishing any good. Still, I had made up my mind that the essay would have to be made, with all the chances against success, or I must abandon the business altogether. Your coming has raised the hope that you can aid me."

CHAPTER XVIII.
PLANNING THE SEARCH.

Harvey Hamilton was about to speak when Detective Pendar raised a warning hand.

"Sh!" he whispered; "some one is in the hall."

The youth listened intently, but could not detect so much as the "shadow of a sound." None the less, his guest was right.

"He has gone by; listen!"

The faintest possible noise, as if made by some one opening and closing a door with the extremest caution, came to their ears.

"It's one of them," remarked the detective, in the same almost inaudible tone; "let's sit as near together as we can, and not raise our voices above a whisper. I allowed you to do so a few minutes ago, because there were no listeners."

"Are those two watchers as you call them staying at the hotel?"

"They occupy the fourth room beyond."

"And my negro lad has the third."

"And I the second; so we are all neighbors."

"How will you manage to leave without detection?"

"I am used to that kind of business," replied Pendar with a smile; "give it no thought. Let us return to the matter in which you are as much interested as I. My proposal is that in sailing over the surrounding country, you scrutinize it, so far as your keen vision, assisted by your binoculars, will permit, in search of the headquarters of this gang."

"How shall I recognize the place if I see it?"

"You will have to follow the law of probabilities. The woods are uninhabited, except in the eastern part—that is, in this direction. If you observe any old house or cabin that shows evidence of being occupied, probably it's the place for which we are looking. Locate it definitely, and then we shall have something upon which to act. As soon as you report to me, I'll move with all the vigor and common sense at my command."

Here was the proposal as clearly as it could be put. Harvey nodded his head several times and compressed his lips, as does one who is in deadly earnest.

"Heaven grant that I shall be able to do something."

"Then I was not wrong in assuming you were interested in the cause of justice?" remarked Detective Pendar.

"Not by a large majority."

"Whoever has a hand in restoring the little girl to her parents will receive a munificent reward. Perhaps this fact may be of interest to you."

"None whatever. Now that I shall undertake the task, we must have an understanding; suppose I discover such a place as you mention, while cruising aloft, how am I to communicate with you without drawing suspicion to myself?"

"There will be no trouble in that. You can return to the hotel, as will be quite natural for you to do, take a room under some pretense such as not feeling well, and I shall get to you without much delay. That done it will not be long before we formulate a plan of action."

"Will my negro prove any handicap to me?"

"On the contrary, I am hoping he will be of help."

"In what way?"

"It is impossible for him to be secretive or cunning; he is so open that his honesty speaks for itself; no one can doubt that you and he are on a little outing, with no purpose except enjoyment."

"You have gauged his character correctly."

"As I did yours."

"Don't be too certain of that; you were correct at least in believing you would enlist my efforts in your work."

"When will you be ready to begin?"

"To-morrow morning,—provided the weather proves as clear as that old farmer declared it would be."

"I heard his prophecy; his neighbors believe him infallible; I think you can count on favoring conditions. Bear in mind that your task is simple. You cannot halt and rest in the air, because you have to travel rapidly to sustain yourself, but you see the enormous advantages your position gives you. Wherever a house, even the smallest one, stands in the woods, the roof or some part of it must be visible from above. The abductors of the child will treat her well so long as there is a prospect of obtaining the ransom, for it is to their interest to do so. There must be cooking done in the dwelling, and the smoke will show; washing and other things are necessary,—all of which you can learn without the aid of glasses from a perch of several hundred feet. Are you acquainted with an aviator known as Professor Morgan?"

The abrupt question startled the youth.

"I met him last night and again this forenoon. He is a crank."

"Rather; his mind is unbalanced, but for all that it is a brilliant intellect which has been knocked topsy-turvy by studying out inventions in aviation."

"And he has made some wonderful ones. He told me he had discovered a chemical which mixed with gasoline will keep him in the air for twelve hours, and he is confident that he will soon double and triple its effectiveness. He has already learned how to sustain his machine for some time motionless."

"Have you seen him do it?"

"I have," and Harvey related the incident of the Professor dropping the giant crackers among the group on the edge of the wood.

"It is a most extraordinary achievement. I suppose he has managed to secure in some way the action of supports which operate like the wings of a bird, when he holds himself stationary in the sky."

"Furthermore, he runs his machine without noise, which is another feat that no one else has been able to attain. It seems to me also that his 'Dragon of the Skies,' as he has named it, can travel faster than the swiftest eagle."

It was in the mind of Harvey to ask the detective how he came to form the acquaintance of Professor Morgan and to inquire whether he knew the crank was in Chesterton at that moment, or had been there during the afternoon; but, as the caller did not volunteer the information, the youth forbore questioning him.

"We shall not forget that whenever and wherever we meet outside of this room, it will be as strangers. If you wish to speak to me on anything, you will take off your cap and scratch your head. If I see that, I shall accept it as notice that you have something important to say. As soon as you can do so without attracting notice you will go to your room. When the coast becomes clear I shall follow you, but prudence may require me to delay doing so for an hour or for several hours."

At that moment both were startled by a loud knock on the door. On the instant, Detective Pendar whispered:

"Make believe you are asleep."

Waiting, therefore, until the summons had been twice repeated, Harvey asked mumblingly:

"Who's there?"

"It's me, Bunk."

"What do you want?"

"Didn't yo' tole me dat I warn't to bodder yo' and yo' would call me in de morning?"

"Of course I did; what's the matter with you?"

"I woke up a little while ago and couldn't disremember for suah what it was yo' tole me, so I slipped to yo' door to find out. Dat's all; good night!"

And his heavy tread sounded along the hall to his door through which he passed. The colored youth had slept so much during the day that he needed little more refreshment of that nature.

"What do you think of that for stupidity?" asked Harvey.

"I am not surprised. I do not recall that I have anything more to say. Will you be good enough to glance up and down the hall in search of anything suspicious?"

The detective himself noiselessly opened the door. Harvey stepped outside and stood listening and gazing toward the rear through the dimly lighted avenue, that being the direction in which the rooms referred to were situated.

"I cannot see or hear anything——"

Turning to face the man whom he addressed, and whom he supposed to be standing directly behind him, Harvey saw nobody. The room was empty. The amazed youth looked the other way, where the stairs lay. He was barely in time to catch a glimpse of his caller in gray as he turned the short corner and disappeared down the steps like a gliding shadow.

"That beats everything," remarked the wondering young aviator, who now locked his door and prepared for bed.

It was a long time, however, after he turned off the light and stretched out on the soft mattress before he was able to woo slumber. Now that the detective had recalled the kidnapping of the Hastings child in Philadelphia, many minor particulars came back to the youth. All these helped to stir his feelings, until he longed for the morning when he could begin his work of bringing the unspeakable miscreants to justice. He comprehended vividly the anguish of those stricken hearts in their luxurious home, and shuddered to think that his own sister Mildred might have been the stolen child.

With his thoughts flitting with lightning rapidity from one subject to another, Harvey regretted that he had not questioned the officer about Professor Morgan. It would be interesting to learn how the two had become acquainted.

"I wonder," added our young friend, following one of his innumerable whimsies, "whether the Professor is on this job too. He seems to be lingering in these parts, and he certainly has advantages which can never be mine. Perhaps when I called to him, he feared it would complicate matters if I was allowed to mix in. What's the use of guessing?" he exclaimed impatiently, as he flung himself on his side and tried for the twentieth time to coax gentle slumber to come to him.

The coquettish goddess consented after a time, though the hour was past midnight when the youth closed his eyes. Such being the situation, it is not strange that Bohunkus Johnson was the first out of bed in the morning, and down stairs. He was thinking of the aeroplane and fearful that it had been molested during the night.

"I orter watched it agin," was his thought as he dashed out of doors.

A few minutes later, Harvey Hamilton was startled by footsteps rushing along the hall, followed by a furious thumping on his door.

"Git up, Harv, quick!" he shouted; "somebody has busted de airyplane all to flinders!"

CHAPTER XIX.
THE AEROPLANE DESTROYED.

With one bound Harvey Hamilton leaped out of bed and jerked open the door. Bohunkus Johnson stood before him, atremble with excitement.

"What is it you say?" demanded the young aviator.

"De airyplane am smashed all to bits! It am kindling wood and nuffin else!" replied the dusky lad, who staggered into the room and dropped into a chair, so overcome that he was barely able to stand.

Never did Harvey dress so quickly. While flinging on his garments, his tongue was busy.

"Have you any idea who did it?"

"Gee! I wish I had! I'd sarve him de same way!"

"Is any one near it?"

"Not a soul; dat is dere wa'n't anyone when I snoke out dere and took a look. Ain't it too bad, Harv? We'll have to walk home."

"We can ride in the cars; that isn't worth thinking about."

Talking in an aimless way, the youths a minute later ran along the hall, skittered down stairs and dashed out to the sheds at the rear of the hotel. The landlord, who was alone in the bar-room, stared wonderingly at them as they shot through the door, but asked no questions.

Bohunkus had scarcely exaggerated in his story. No aeroplane that gave out in the upper regions and slanted downward to rocky earth was ever more utterly wrecked. One or more persons had evidently used a heavy axe to work the destruction. Both wings had been smashed, fully two-thirds of the ribs being splintered; the lever handles were broken and even the two blades of the propeller had been shattered. The machine had been hacked in other places. The engine, carbureter and magneto were about all that remained intact, and even they showed dents and bruises as if attempts had been made to destroy them.

Harvey walked sadly around the ruin and viewed it from every angle. His face was pale, for his indignation was stirred to the profoundest depths. He said nothing until his companion asked:

"Who'd you think done it?"

"I have no more idea than the man in the moon. There may have been only one person, or there may have been half a dozen. Ah, if I knew!"

Several men straggled into the open yard and to the shed where they gathered about the two youths. Harvey looked around and saw there were six, with others coming into sight. Somehow or other the news of such outrages seems to travel by a system of wireless telegraphy of their own. In a short time a score of spectators were gathered, all asking questions and making remarks.

The thought struck Harvey that among this group were probably the criminals. He looked into their faces and compressing his lips said:

"I'll give a hundred dollars to learn what scoundrel did this."

"I'll gib fourteen million," added Bohunkus enthusiastically.

A tall, stoop-shouldered young man shook his head.

"Whoever he was he oughter be lynched and I'd like to help do it."

The suspicion entered the mind of the young aviator that it was not at all unlikely that the speaker was the guilty one. With him might have been joined others and Harvey studied their faces in the hope of gaining a clue, but in vain. Knowing his father would back his action he said:

"That was done by some person in Chesterton; you know the people better than I do; if you would like to earn two hundred dollars find who he or they were."

Something in the nature of a reaction came over our young friend. Ashamed of his weakness, he turned his back on the group, walked rapidly to the hotel and went to his room. And it must be confessed that when he reached that, he sat down in his chair, covered his face with his hands and sobbed as if his heart were broken. Bohunkus, who was at his heels, faced him in another chair, and unable to think of anything appropriate for the occasion, held his peace, frequently crossing and uncrossing his beam-like legs, clenching his fists and sighing. He yearned to do something, but couldn't decide what it should be.

Harvey's outburst lasted only a brief while. He washed his face and deliberately completed his toilet.

"There's no use of crying over spilt milk, Bunk," he remarked calmly; "let's go down to breakfast."

"I knowed dere was something I'd forgot,—and dat's it. Seems to me I'm allers hungry, Harv."

"I have thought that a good many times."

"I'll tell you what we'll do, so's to git rewenge on 'em."

"What's that?" asked Harvey, who, as is sometimes the case in mental stress, felt an almost morbid interest in trifles.

"Let's eat up eberything in de house, so de rest ob de people will starve to def; de willain dat done dat will be among 'em and dat's de way we'll get eben wid him."

"You might be able, Bunk, to carry out your plan, but I couldn't give you much help. Come on and I'll try to think out what is the best thing to do."

The second descent of the boys was a contrast to their first. They showed little or no trace of agitation, as they walked into the dining-room and sat down at the long table where three other guests had preceded them. Harvey was so disturbed that he ate only a few mouthfuls, but hardly less than an earthquake would have affected the appetite of his companion.

In turning over in his mind the all-absorbing question, Harvey Hamilton could think of only one explanation. He believed the destruction of his aeroplane was due to simple wantonness, for many a man and boy do mischief just because it is mischief and they know such action is wrong on their part. It was impossible that he should have an enemy in this country town. It might be the guilty one or ones were actuated by an unreasoning jealousy or a superstitious belief that the strange machine was likely to inflict evil upon the community.

Something like this we say was his theory, though he was not entirely rid of a vague belief that some other cause might exist. This was an occasion when he needed the aid of the detective, Simmons Pendar, who was not in the dining-room nor had he seen him about the hotel. In the hope of discovering his friend Harvey strolled into the sitting-room and took the seat he had occupied the day before. The man in gray was invisible, as were the two foreign looking individuals who were under suspicion by the officer.

The question which the young aviator was asking himself was as to the right course for him to follow. Deprived in this summary fashion of his air machine, he was without power of giving Pendar any help in his attempt to recover little Grace Hastings from the kidnappers. Any essay on his part in that direction, now that he was confined to earth, was sure to hinder more than to aid.

He was still in a maze of perplexity when Bohunkus came ponderously to his feet and started through the door connecting with the hall which led up stairs. Harvey naturally looked up to learn why he did so. With the door drawn back and the negro in the act of stepping across the threshold, he turned his head, grinned and winked at his friend. Then he passed out, closing the door behind him, and the mystified Harvey heard his muffled footsteps along the hall and ascending the stairs.

"What can he be driving at?" Harvey asked himself; "that wink looked as if it was an invitation for me to follow him."

Thus early in the day the two were the only ones in the sitting-room, so that no one could have noticed the action of the two. Nor is it easy to understand why Bohunkus should have relied upon a wink of the eye, when it was as easy and would have been much clearer had he used his gift of speech; but we know how fond his race are of mystery.

When Harvey reached the top of the stairs, where the view was unobstructed along the hall, he saw Bunk standing at his door, as if waiting for him. The space between the two was such that this time the dusky youth instead of winking flirted his head. Then he stepped into Harvey's room and stood just beyond the partially open door and awaited his friend.

Harvey did not forget that they were near the apartment of Detective Pendar as well as that of the suspected parties, and while moving along the passage way he did his utmost in the way of looking and listening. He made no attempt to soften the noise of his footsteps, for that of itself would have betrayed him. He strode forward and through the doors and stood beside the waiting Bohunkus, who stealthily turned the key in the lock. Then he beckoned to Harvey to bring his chair and place it alongside the one in which the African softly seated himself on the far side of the room.

By this time the white youth was beginning to lose patience.

"What is the matter with you, Bunk?"

"Sh! not so loud," replied the other, placing a forefinger against his bulbous lips.

"Use a little common sense if you have such a thing about you. If you don't speak out and explain things, you must get out of my room."

"All right den; Harv, I know who smashed yo' airyplane!"

"You do! Why didn't you tell me before?"

"Wanted to break it to yo' gentle like."

"Who was it?" demanded the astounded youth.

"Perfesser Morgan!"

Harvey stared in amazement for a moment and then asked:

"How do you know it was he who did it?"

"I seed him!"

"Are you crazy or only a fool, Bunk? Explain yourself. Do you mean to tell me that you saw Professor Morgan destroy my aeroplane?"

"Didn't perzactly see him doot, but I seed 'nough."

"How much did you see?"

"When I fust went out ob de hotel and round de corner in de yard by de sheds I seed a tall man, wid his long linen duster, slip fru dat place where two boards had been ripped off. Jes' as he was slipping fru, he turned and looked at me; dere was de long part-gray whiskers and de black debilish eyes. Oh, it war him and no mistake, Harv," added Bohunkus with an air of finality.

CHAPTER XX.
A PUZZLING TELEGRAM.

Harvey Hamilton was astounded. In all his imaginings he had never dreamed of this explanation of the destruction of his aeroplane. One admirable trait of the thick-witted Bohunkus Johnson was his truthfulness. His friend knew he was not trying to deceive him and what he had told could be accepted as fact.

"Why did you wait so long, Bunk, before telling me this story?"

"Wal, Harv, I didn't want to 'bleve it myself; I didn't at first,—dat is, I didn't think de Perfesser was as mean as all dat, but it was him and no mistake."

"I am sure you are right, though I can't understand why he should do such a thing."

"Guess he war jealous ob us."

"Possibly so, but even then it is hard to understand."

Harvey still refrained from giving the obvious explanation that presented itself. A man who is mentally unbalanced cannot be held accountable for his acts. It was impossible to feel the resentment toward Professor Morgan which he would have felt had the man been in his right mind. Harvey sighed.

"Only one thing remains for us to do, Bunk."

"What is that?"

"Go home and give up our outing. Hist! some one is coming."

Footsteps were heard ascending the stairs. Whoever the person was, he came with deliberate tread along the hall, and halting in front of the door, knocked smartly. Harvey sprang to his feet and opened. The landlord stood before him.

"Here's a telegram for you; I signed; nothing to pay."

The wondering youth accepted the yellow envelope and tore it open. He read:

"Go to Groveton and wait. You will learn something to your advantage."

"GABRIEL HAMILTON."

The message was dated at his father's place of business in New York, and as shown was signed by him.

"There is no answer," said Harvey to the waiting landlord, who departed.

"This is beyond me," he remarked after reading the telegram to Bohunkus, who of course was as much mystified as his companion. "Why we should go to Groveton and what is there that can be of advantage to me, is a greater puzzle than the wrecking of the aeroplane."

"What am yo' gwine to do, Harv?"

"Obey orders. Come on."

The two traveled with so light baggage that they had only to fling their extra coats over their arms, the few minor articles being in their pockets, and descend the stairs. Harvey paid his bill and explained that he had been called suddenly away by the telegram from his father, but it was possible he might return. The landlord expressed his sympathy for the loss of the aeroplane and promised to do all he could to find out who the criminals were.

"Don't bother," said Harvey airily, "it's lucky it didn't happen when we were a mile or two up in the sky."

"I understand that you will pay a reward of two hundred dollars for the detection of the scamps?"

"Yes, the offer stands," replied Harvey, confident that the really guilty individual would never be discovered. "You have my address on your register; if you learn anything, write or telegraph me. By the way, how far is Groveton from here?"

"Twelve miles by railroad."

"Is it much of a town?"

"Not quite as big as Chesterton."

"What time can we leave for the place?"

The landlord glanced at the clock behind him.

"If you walk briskly you can catch the next train."

Harvey engaged the man to take care of the remains of the aeroplane during his absence, and having been directed as to the right course, the two hurried along the single street and turned off to the station on their right. They were just in time to buy tickets and take their seats. Their course was to the westward, which was the direction of the wide valley between the mountainous ridges. Twenty minutes later they stepped out on the platform and inquired the name of the nearest hotel. As in the town they had just left, there was only one hostelry, the Rawlins Hotel, to which they made their way.

Wondering and perplexed to the last degree, Harvey entered the place of board and lodging. He explained that he did not know how long he would stay, and as it was only the middle of the forenoon, he did not register, saying he would do so at noon, in the event of his remaining that long.

The day was so pleasant—the prophecy of the weather prophet having been fulfilled to the letter—that they sat down on the long bench which ran along the front of the hotel, and waited for whatever might turn up.

"If any one is to meet me, he would come here," reflected Harvey; "I can't imagine who he is or what news he will bring, but I shall learn in due time."

A half hour later, while the two were seated side by side, occasionally making a guess as to what it all meant, which guess both knew was wide of the mark, Bohunkus said:

"Seems to me dem folks out dere am looking at something."

Excitement was fast spreading through the town. Groups stood on the corners, halted in the middle of the street and at every coign of advantage. All were peering into the sky, where some object attracted their attention. Naturally Harvey and Bohunkus rose from their seats and passed out to the front where their view was clear.

"Gee! it am anoder airyplane!" exclaimed the negro.

"You are right; they seem to be growing plentiful in this part of the world."

"Wonder if it am de Perfesser."

Harvey whipped his binoculars around and leveled them at the object, whose outstretched wings identified it as one of the most modern ships of the air. A brief scrutiny showed that it was not the extraordinary invention of that extraordinary man who had crossed their path more than once. It was a biplane, and though still a considerable distance away the noise of its motor was audible. It was traveling fast and heading for the little town of Groveton.

It was evident that whoever was guiding the aerial craft was an expert. Harvey saw that it carried only the operator, who described a large circle over the town at a height of nearly a thousand feet and then began descending.

"He's gwine to land here!" exclaimed Bunk.

"And has picked out his spot," added Harvey.

Such proved to be the fact. There was a broad, open space in front of the Rawlins House, where a large number of teams could find room, the area being such as to offer an ideal spot for the landing of an aeroplane. The aviator, who was now seen to be a youth not much if any older than Harvey himself, guided his machine with consummate skill, and lightly touched the ground within fifty feet of where our young friends and half a hundred others were standing. The aeroplane ran a few yards on its wheels, and then came to a halt. The young man stepped lightly to the ground and smilingly greeted the crowd. His next words were:

"I am looking for Harvey Hamilton and his colored companion."

"Dat's us," whispered the startled Bohunkus.

Harvey stepped forward.

"That is my name; what do you wish with me?"

"I have orders to hand over this biplane to you."

"To me!" repeated Harvey, who felt as if wonders would never cease; "why to me?"

"Your father, Mr. Gabriel Hamilton, ordered it by telegraph to be sent here this morning. I understand your machine has been wrecked."

"It has, but how did you learn it?"

The handsome youth smiled as he offered his hand.

"I am Paul Mitchell, from Garden City; we received a telegram from your father this morning asking us to send a biplane to you at once, as yours had been knocked out of commission. We happened to have one ready and I started right off and have made pretty good time to this spot in Pennsylvania."

"I should say you had, for it is several hundred miles from Long Island; but how in the name of the seven wonders did father come to know of my mishap?"

Young Mitchell laughed.

"He gave no explanation, but some one must have told him."

"Who could it have been?"

"I give it up."

"Were you asked to come to Groveton?"

"No; Chesterton was given as the place where your misfortune overtook you. Since I did not know the particulars, our folks thought it best I should meet you at some point not far from there. In replying to your father's telegram, I stated this, which explains why he repeated the name to you."

"But not where he got his knowledge."

"Let that question go till you meet him, when he will make it clear. What caused the breakage of your machine?"

"Somebody chopped it up; it was done in spite."

"Did you catch the scoundrel?"

"Catch him! no; nobody knows where he is."

"Well, such things happen and it is all a part of the game. Suppose we go to Chesterton, and have a look at the remains; there must be some salvage which I can ship to the factory. How about the engine?"

"It is battered, but must be worth repairing."

"If you and your friend will seat yourselves, I shall have you there in a jiffy."

Bohunkus and Harvey climbed into the seat and adjusted themselves. Young Mitchell examined the different parts of the biplane, which was an almost exact replica of the one that had been wrecked, and then took charge of the business. At his request one of the bystanders swung the blades of the propeller around so as to start the motor, and several held on until the tugging almost drew them off their feet. Then they let go, and away sailed the second machine for Chesterton.

CHAPTER XXI.
BEGINNING THE SEARCH.

There certainly had been lively work, for within six hours after the discovery of the destroyed aeroplane, a message had been sent from New York to Garden City, Long Island, a machine despatched from that point to the little town among the Alleghanies in eastern Pennsylvania, and an aerial ship had sailed across the State of New Jersey to the destination more than two hundred miles from its starting point. When and by what means the merchant had learned of the straits of his son could not as yet be guessed, but the news must have been waiting when he reached his office in the city, since young Mitchell said it was received at the factory between eight and nine o'clock that morning. The flight to Groveton was made in about four hours, with a brief halt on the way to replenish the supply of gasoline. Traveling at the rate of fifty miles an hour and sometimes faster was surely "going some."

As Mitchell afterward explained, he had visited the section twice, and was familiar with it. He lost no time, therefore, in groping, but recognized rivers, cities, towns, and the general conformation of the country over which he glided, and identified Groveton long before any one there dreamed he intended to make a call.

Harvey glanced at the little watch on his wrist, and noted the exact time of starting. Eleven minutes later to the second, he volplaned into the open space in front of the hotel. Although the distance passed was less than by rail, he must have averaged nearly if not quite a mile a minute.

The lesson of the "accident" to the other machine was not lost upon the two young men. It was hardly to be supposed that any one would try to harm the new one, but Bohunkus was ordered to stay with it and see that all hands were kept off.

"Yo' bet I will," he replied, fully alive to his duty; "de fust chap dat lays an onkind hand on dis pet will git broke in 'leben pieces and den flung ober de fence."

Several idlers were gaping at the fractured aeroplane huddled in the wagon sheds of the hotel. Mitchell quickly finished his examination.

"The man or men who did that," he said in a low voice to Harvey, "showed the devil's own spite. It looks as if the scoundrel was crazy."

Harvey glanced at his companion. Did he suspect the truth? His looks and manner, however, showed that he was not thinking of Professor Morgan. The remark was a natural one, under the circumstances. Harvey was not disposed to reveal anything, since he saw no good to be accomplished thereby, while an unpleasant situation might develop.

"You can save something out of the wreck?" remarked the owner inquiringly.

"Considerable; I shall ship what's worth while to the factory at Garden City, and in a few weeks you will have a new machine as good as ever."

"The greater part of it will have to be new," commented Harvey.

"That being so, you can return this one in exchange, if you wish."

"Is there any way, Mitchell, in which I can serve you?"

"None; I shall have what is left of the machine gathered up, as I said, and sent to the factory; that will take the remainder of the day, when I shall follow in the train. Meanwhile you are not called upon to lose any part of your vacation. There is no perceptible difference between the two biplanes, so you don't need any help from me."

The youths walked back to where a small group remained staring at the biplane in which Bohunkus Johnson was still seated, as alert as a watch dog. As the couple approached, the negro crooked his stubby forefinger to his friend, who went forward.

"What is it, Bunk?"

"Yo's forgot something."

"What is that?"

"It's 'bout dinner time."

The colored youth meant to whisper, but his husky aspiration carried as far as if he had spoken in a loud tone.

"He is right," remarked Mitchell; "let us have dinner together."

The old fellow who served the hotel as hostler was hired to stay by the machine and to keep every other person at a distance, while the three went in to their meal.

During these minutes, Harvey was on the watch for a sight of Detective Pendar. He much wanted to have a few words with him, but was puzzled how to bring it about. Harvey had given up his room, so he could not signal to the officer to follow him thither and there was no understanding as to how they should otherwise meet.

Pendar, however, remained invisible until Bohunkus had perched himself in the seat in front of the tank, and Harvey had his hands on the levers. Mitchell stepped to the rear to give a swing to the propeller blades. The machine was pointed to the left, where the highway showed quite a sharp slope downward, of which the young aviator meant to take advantage.

At this crisis, when twenty pairs of eyes were upon the party, Harvey heard an odd sounding cough. He looked around and saw a man standing on the porch above the other spectators. It was Detective Pendar, who was looking keenly at Harvey. As their eyes met the former rubbed his smooth chin thoughtfully and winked once, but made no other sign that he recognized the youth.

"Now what does he mean by that?" Harvey asked himself; "a wink may signify one of a score of things." As the only reply he could make, he winked in return. A dozen of the group might have accepted it as meant for him, but, if so, he must have been equally puzzled with the author of the signal, who a minute later was scooting through the air and steadily rising.

Harvey had decided to carry out so far as he could the programme agreed upon the day before by him and Pendar. The only change was that caused by the enforced delay. Instead of making his search in the forenoon, it now would have to be done in the afternoon. He shot upward, until barely five hundred feet above the earth, and then headed westward over the long stretch of forest of which mention has been made. It was advisable that he should keep as near the ground as practical, since his view would thereby be improved.

Bohunkus Johnson was still in the dark on two points: he had no conception of the serious business upon which his companion was engaged, knowing nothing of the kidnapped child, and, though certain in his own mind that Professor Morgan was the man who had wrecked the aeroplane, he had never suspected that he was insane. Ignorance on the former point was a good thing, but as regards the latter it proved a serious mistake, as has been intimated in another place.

It need not be said that a heavier-than-air machine must progress rapidly in order to sustain itself aloft. When such motion stops, through breakage, accident or the will of the aviator, an aeroplane obeys the law of gravity and comes to the ground. It does not fall, as is the case with a balloon.

It would never do to withdraw care from the machine, which worked with perfect smoothness, but having headed westward and struck as moderate a gait as was practical, Harvey Hamilton gave all the attention possible to the country under his feet. He noted the wide expanse of forest in its exuberant foliage, a flashing stream of water and the foam of a tumbling cascade on the slope of the farther ridge. In the other direction wound the railway line over which he and Bunk had ridden earlier in the day. The sky was clear and sunshiny with a rift of fleecy clouds in advance, but at so great an elevation that no inconvenience was to be feared from them. The town of Groveton was so distinctly seen that he recognized several of the buildings, including the hotel, which he had observed on his brief visit. Far away in the radiant horizon the steeples and tall buildings of a city showed, but it was all strange to him. He could identify nothing beyond that which has been named.

Harvey had sailed probably three or four miles from Chesterton when he was thrilled by a sight that roused instant hope. In the midst of the wood, an open space several acres in extent was crossed by a stream of considerable size, on its winding way to the distant Delaware. In the center of this clearing stood a log cabin, which recalled that of Abisha Wharton where Harvey and Bunk had spent a night after leaving home on their outing. The land showed slight signs of cultivation, but from the stone chimney running up the outside of the decayed structure, he traced a faint blue spiral of smoke.

IN THE CENTER STOOD A LOG CABIN.

"That shows somebody lives there," was Harvey's thought; "from what Pendar told me I believe it's the very place where the kidnappers are holding the child a prisoner."

He leaned far over and scrutinized the picture as he swept over it. What he longed to see was the little girl running about or playing in front of the cabin, or one or more of her captors. It would seem that the loud throbbing of his motor ought to have attracted the attention of the occupants, but it did not do so, and the spot speedily glided from sight. When Harvey twisted his neck, however, in the effort to see more, he noticed that Bunk had also turned and was attentively studying the picture. Conversation in such circumstances was impossible, but Harvey hoped his companion had discovered something—a supposition which he was certain to remember when the time came for a halt in their flight.

Had our young friend followed his inclination, he would have circled around and returned over the cabin, in order to inspect it further, but that most likely would have roused the suspicion of the abductors, and the moment they believed an aeroplane had been impressed into the service against them, that moment the usefulness of the contrivance would be ended. He could remember the location clearly, and would give the detective all the directions he needed.

"I didn't see any wagon road or trails, but there must be one path at least which connects the house with the outer world. Those men have a source of supplies and they can't help leaving footprints."

As Harvey reasoned out the problem, the solution was simplified. Simmons Pendar was confident that the hiding place was somewhere in the stretch of wilderness, but to search for it would prove fatal. The effort was certain of discovery by the watchful guards. Now, however, since the exact location of the cabin seemed to have been found, a speedy approach ought to be within the detective's power. The near future must answer the question.

CHAPTER XXII.
IN DANGER OF COLLISION.

The cabin in the clearing being no longer in Harvey Hamilton's field of vision, he gave his attention to the management of his aeroplane. In order to avoid so far as possible arousing suspicion, he made a sweeping bend to the northward, with a view of passing over the ridge and then returning to Chesterton from the east. By following this course, he would make it impossible for the tenants of the log cabin to see him, and thus render distrust on their part out of the question.

It was important that he should remain over night in Chesterton, in order to report to Detective Pendar and receive instructions from him. The youth was morbidly sensitive about offending the gentleman, or doing anything that could interfere with the success of the extraordinary enterprise in which he was engaged.

Harvey had changed the course of the machine and lifted the edge of his front rudder in order to make sure of clearing the top of the ridge, when Bohunkus touched him smartly with the toe of his shoe. The aviator turned his head to learn the cause, and the dusky youth with staring eyes pointed to the northwest, that is somewhat to the left of the course they were following. Looking in that direction, Harvey to his astonishment saw an aeroplane no more than a mile distant. With a minute or two at his disposal, he brought his binoculars into play.

The first glance told him an amazing fact.

"As sure as I'm alive, it's the Dragon of the Skies! Professor Morgan is coming this way too! I'll be neighborly and meet him."

The vertical rudder at the rear was shifted, and the two machines the next moment were so headed that a collision threatened unless one changed its course.

Bohunkus kicked the shoulder of his friend again. His dark face revealed his terror.

"He's gwine to smash dis locumotive! What'll 'come ob us?"

Of course not a syllable of these words could be heard in the thunderous throbbing of the motor, but the expression of Bunk's face and the vigorous contortions of his lips made his meaning clear. It occurred to Harvey that there might be cause for his companion's alarm. There is no accounting for the whimsies of a crank, and, having destroyed one aeroplane, what more likely than that he should wreak his fury upon another, particularly when it was handled by the owner of the former?

Harvey's first inclination was to shift his course again and run away from the Professor, but he reflected that if he did so, he would invite pursuit, and speedy as was the new machine it was certain the Dragon of the Skies was speedier. An inventor who was able to construct an "uplifter" that would hold his monoplane as stationary as a bird waiting for sight of the fish far below before making its dive, or could muffle his motor into noiselessness without lessening its power, was sure, beside doing all this, to acquire a speed that no rival could equal.

It was better to put a bold face on the situation, and paying no heed, therefore, to the gestures and mute shouts of his companion, Harvey headed for the monoplane, which approached with the speed and accuracy of an arrow.

Less than two hundred yards separated the two when Professor Morgan veered to the right, curving so far that his course shifted to a right angle of the other machine, toward which he turned broadside.

There sat the strange man in plain view, his feet on the cross-piece below, his hands resting on the upright levers, between which he sat bolt upright, with his linen duster buttoned from chin to ankles, his cap drawn low, while those blazing black eyes above his grizzled beard suggested an owl peering through a thicket and were turned full upon the two youths in the biplane.

Harvey waved his hand in salutation, but the Professor did not seem to see him or Bunk. He glided past, and when he had shot beyond a point opposite, turned his head so as to look directly in front. Harvey gave him no further notice, for he was now so near the ridge that all his skill was needed to direct his aeroplane.

Bohunkus was not yet free from his shivering fear, and kept his eye upon the dreaded Professor.

"I know what de willain am up to," he reflected; "he's only makin' b'lieve dat he's gwine to lebe us. He'll snoke round behind and de fust thing we know will be when dat rudder out in front jams into us, slides under me, lifts me out ob dis seat and pitches me head fust down among dem treetops."

But the form of the Dragon of the Skies grew smaller and fainter until the aching eyes of the negro could see it no longer. By that time the watcher concluded that nothing for the present was to be feared from the eccentric individual.

"But we hain't done wid him yit," said Bunk; "he's got his eye on us, for if he hadn't why am he hangin' round de country, bobbin' up when we ain't lookin' fur him? He'll find out where we're gwine to stay to-night and den he'll get a new axe as big as de side ob a house and smash dis machine wuss dan de oder. De Perfesser am mighty sly and I doan' like him; I wish he'd take a shine to some oder part ob de world."

Having surmounted the ridge, Harvey sailed ten or more miles to the northward and descended at a town containing probably ten thousand population. There he renewed his supply of gasoline and oil, and halted for an hour or so, when he was prepared to return to Chesterton. While he and Bohunkus were seated apart from the others at the hotel, the colored youth gave voice to his dissatisfaction.

"What's de use ob hangin' round dis part ob de country, Harv? How many times do yo' expect to go to Chesterton?"

"I have some business there to attend to. When that is finished, we can travel as far as you wish in any direction."

"Why can't we go to Afriky?" was the astounding question.

Harvey laughed.

"Why, Bunk, that is thousands of miles off. We should have to cross the Atlantic Ocean."

"What's to hender doing dat?"

"You know we have to renew our supply of gasoline and oil every few hours. Can you tell me how it is possible to do it when hundreds of miles from land? We spoke of this before."

"Don't de ships and steamboats carry de stuff?"

"If we could count upon meeting one of them when needed, we might get on, but when father and I crossed the ocean, we passed days at a time without seeing a sail."

"Hang a boat on to de bottom of dis keer and paddle till we run agin a ship."

"Drive that wild idea out of your head, Bunk. I don't doubt that you and I shall live to see the day when aeroplanes will make regular trips between the continents, but we must wait till that time comes."

"Doan' yo' spose Perfesser Morgan can doot?"

"He has made so many wonderful inventions, he may be the first to succeed. When he does, we shall hear of it."

Bohunkus was silent for a minute or so. If his friend had imagined what wild freak had entered the lad's brain, he would have made all haste to root it out, but unfortunately he did not dream of anything of the kind.

The next query of Bunk was more startling to Harvey than anything that had gone before.

"Harv, did yo' see dat little girl?"

"What do you mean?" demanded the other sharply.

"When we was sailing ober dem woods, after we'd left Chesterton."

"I saw no little girl; did you?"

"Sartinously; yo' doan' forgot dat cabin down among the trees where a small creek runs in front ob it."

This was unquestionably the place in which Harvey had been so much interested. He had not observed a living person near it, while his dusky companion had seen the very person that was in many minds.

"I saw the old house and the smoke coming out of the chimney, but did not catch sight of a man, woman or child. Tell me how it was with you."

"Nuffin 'ticular; we'd got a little way beyont and you wasn't looking back when I took a notion to turn my head. Dere warn't any man or woman in sight, but a little gal was standin' in front ob de door, a wavin' her handkerchief at me. I took off my cap and swinged it at her, but we was too fur off and de ingine made too much noise for us to hold a conwersation."

"This is very interesting, Bunk."

Remembering the instructions of Detective Pendar, Harvey gave no hint of why he felt so much concern over what had just been told him. The slow wits of Bohunkus were likely to cause trouble and probably defeat the delicate plans which the officer of the law had in mind. What the colored youth had told removed the last vestige of doubt from the young aviator as to the identity of the cabin of which he had caught a passing glimpse. He felt certain that the little girl whom Bohunkus saw and with whom he exchanged salutations was Grace Hastings, kidnapped weeks before, and for whose recovery her father was spending a fortune. Harvey knew the exact spot where she was a prisoner and could direct the detective unerringly to it. He was eager to do so, for his heart was enlisted in the sacred task.

In his desire to do something effective, Harvey was on the point of setting out again with his aeroplane and taking a course that would lead him over the cabin in the clearing. He wished to gain another view of it, and particularly of the child whose absence had plunged her parents in anguish more poignant than if they had looked upon her pale innocent face in death.

But the youth was impressed with the necessity of using the utmost care with every step he took. If he sailed over the cabin again, the fact was likely to be noticed by the men in the structure. If they had not already observed the aeroplane, they had learned of its flight from the chatter of the young captive, and should it return within a few hours would mean something out of the ordinary. It would cause a change of quarters at once and place the recovery of the child beyond attainment.

"There is only one safe thing for me to do," was his decision; "I must take so roundabout course to Chesterton that no one in the cabin will know of it. I shall wait in the town till I can have a talk with Pendar. I have done all he asked of me and from this point forward, under heaven everything depends upon him."

CHAPTER XXIII.
THE CABIN IN THE WOODS.

Twilight had come when Harvey Hamilton, with Bohunkus Johnson seated behind him, descended in the same spot in Chesterton that he had used upon his disastrous visit of the night before. A similar crowd greeted him, and he hired several of their number to drag the aeroplane to the primitive hangar in which the wrecked one had been sheltered.

He learned that Paul Mitchell had shipped the engine and other valuable parts to Garden City, while the shattered framework had been piled to one side to serve as kindling wood for the hotel. Thus vanished one aeroplane to be succeeded speedily by another. Harvey announced that he intended to stay until the morrow. He first engaged two reliable men, upon the recommendation of the landlord, to stay by the machine all night, with instructions to challenge any one who approached and to shoot if necessary.

"We'll likely shoot first and challenge afterward," remarked one with a grin; "I only hope the same fellow will try his hand on this that splintered t'other one."

Nine guests were at supper, that being the name of the meal which was served at the close of the day. One of them was Simmons Pendar, who hardly glanced in the direction of Harvey Hamilton seated opposite. The youth made no attempt to catch his eye, though aware that the detective glanced at him several times. When certain the action would be observed, the young aviator committed a breach of decorum by deliberately scratching his head with one hand. While this was not the precise telegram that had been agreed upon the night before, it was sufficiently to the point, and Harvey was confident it had accomplished its purpose.

The two lads lingered at the table after Pendar and most of the others had left the dining hall. Then they strolled outside on the porch, where by that time the full moon was shining in an unclouded sky. The air was so balmy and soft that few lingered indoors. The gas had been lighted in the sitting-room to which Harvey sauntered, and mosquitoes and other insects hovered in the glare. Three men were seated in lounging positions, one smoking a cigarette, while the others nodded as if yielding to drowsiness. Harvey identified two as having been present when the bit of paper was flipped upon the pad he was using for his crude sketches. The three looked like drummers, but a couple were distinctively foreign in appearance. One had a black curled mustache, with eyes and hair of midnight hue, a second was almost as dark, while the third was an unmistakable blond. They appeared to be unacquainted with one another, but Harvey was almost certain that two if not the three were the men who were watching Pendar while he in turn was keeping them under scrutiny. The officer, however, was nowhere to be seen and the youth did not think it prudent to make any search for him.

"I think I'll go to my room," he remarked, rising to his feet with a yawn; "we have had a pretty strenuous day and shall want to leave early to-morrow."

"All right," grunted Bohunkus; "I feels sorter sleepy myself, and if dese blamed 'skeeters don't lebe me alone I'll tumble into bed likewise."

As Harvey passed out of the door, he carelessly lifted his cap and scratched his head, thus making the full signal previously arranged. He still failed to see the detective and doubted whether he was near.

The youth did not light the gas in his room, though he lacked the pretext of wishing to keep out the insects, since each window was furnished with a screen. He sat down and listened.

Fifteen minutes later, without the slightest preliminary warning, a soft, almost inaudible tap sounded on the door. He drew it noiselessly inward, and recognized the form of Detective Pendar against the soft yellow background. Neither spoke at first. The caller shoved the door shut and with extreme care turned the key. Then he whispered:

"Let's take the other side of the room."

Carrying their chairs thither they placed them side by side. Enough illumination came through the transom for them dimly to discern each other.

"You caught on at the table?" remarked Harvey inquiringly.

"Of course; I noticed your signal, too, when you walked out of the sitting-room."

"Where were you?"

"On the porch, with my eyes on you. I knew you wished to speak with me, but I preferred first to receive your notice."

"I caught your wink to-day when about to start off with my new machine, but I couldn't guess what you meant."

"I meant nothing except to wish you good luck; of course I was aware what you had set out to do and I shall be glad to know what success you met."

"Far better than I expected; I found the place."

"You mean where the little girl is held a prisoner?"

"Yes."

Harvey was surprised that the detective did not show excitement over the news. He remained cool and deliberate and spoke in low-toned words as before.

"Then you saw the child?"

"No, but I sailed over the house."

"How do you know the child is there?"

"Bohunkus, my colored companion, saw her just after we had passed and waved his cap in reply to her salutation with her handkerchief."

"Did he see any of the men?"

"No; they kept out of sight, at least so long as we could have seen them."

"How did your boy describe the girl?"

"He didn't describe her," replied Harvey, a bit chagrined over the pointed questions, "except to say she was a little girl."

"Didn't tell how she was dressed or how old she appeared to be? The last might have been hard to answer, but he should have noticed her apparel."

"Probably he did, but I did not think of asking him."

"It was hardly necessary," remarked the detective, as if regretting his incisive queries. "Now, if you will be good enough to locate the spot I shall be infinitely obliged."

Harvey was able to do this with so much accuracy that his friend complimented him.

"You have done remarkably well; if we succeed in restoring the child to her parents, much of the credit will be due you. I know the exact spot and can go to it without trouble."

"Will you do so?"

"I shall make the effort, but I am in a delicate situation. You noticed those three men in the sitting-room when you were there a little while ago. Two are members of the Black Hand and are acting as scouts."

"I set down all three as being such."

"The blond has nothing to do with the others. He is a genuine commercial traveler for a Philadelphia clothing house and will leave to-morrow. It is the others who belong to the worst gang in the country."

"Do you think they have any suspicion of me?"

Detective Pendar chuckled softly.

"Why should they? You have not given the first cause."

"But they suspect you?"

"I can say I have reason to hope not; I have behaved so well and sold so much hardware stuff in this town that they ought to believe I am what I pretend to be."

"What further help can I give you, Mr. Pendar?"

"None, so far as I see at this moment. But you mustn't minimize your share; the location of the prison is a great and invaluable exploit of itself."

"What will you next do?"

"It is impossible to say, so much depends upon circumstances as they develop."

This answer was so vague that it reminded Harvey he was asking questions which he had not the right to ask. The man before him was a professional detective, whose calling required him to be secretive. While such persons often reveal their secrets in stories, they are the last ones in the world to do so in real life.

"I need not remind you," he continued, "not to drop a hint of these matters to your colored companion."

"I shall not forget your warning on that point. He means well, but in some respects he is as stupid as a child of five years. What do you think?"

asked Harvey with a light laugh, "he asked me to start with him and the aeroplane for Africa to call on his father, Chief Bohunkus Foozleum."

"He may make the journey yet," was the remarkable response of the detective.

"Do you think it possible?"

"Not yet, but it isn't safe to declare anything impossible in our twentieth century. This navigation of the air will make miraculous advancements in the next ten years. Well," abruptly added the caller, "if the coast is clear, I must bid you good night."

"When shall I see you again?" asked Harvey.

"Will you return to Chesterton to-morrow?"

"Is it advisable?"

"I see no objection to your doing so. If you do, and I am here, we may signal each other as before. I'll raise my hat and scratch my head as notice that I wish to have a talk with you in your room, and you will do the same with me if necessary. Please keep your seat."

Harvey saw the dim figure move across the room like a shadow. Pendar waited two or three minutes with his hand on the knob, as if he had heard something, though the listening youth did not detect the slightest sound. Then the door opened as noiselessly as before and he vanished into the hall, leaving the same dead quiet behind him.

Harvey waited some time before preparing for bed. Then he gave expression to his impatience with himself:

"He got everything I knew about this business from me, and I didn't worm a single fact from him. I meant to ask his opinion of the wrecking of my machine, how father learned so early of it, what course Pendar means to follow, and lots of other things, but I know no more than before he came into the room. There's one thing certain, he understands his business through and through, and I don't know the a-b-c of it."

CHAPTER XXIV.
ON THE TRAIL OF THE BLACK HANDERS.

Simmons Pendar had the reputation of being one of the best officers in the detective service. Several of his exploits proved that he possessed a brilliant mind, was quick in reading the vaguest clues and marvelously successful in following them up. It is not my purpose to explain by what subtle means he convinced himself that the kidnappers of little Grace Hastings had their headquarters in the extensive wilderness to the westward of the country town of Chesterton. Had he confessed the truth he would have admitted that a trifling occurrence, one of those insignificant incidents which figure oftener than is believed in important matters, gave him the key. Being human like the rest of us, he made his mistakes now and then, but felt absolutely sure he had not blundered in the present instance.

Pendar shared his secret with no one. The surety of a magnificent money reward, the glory of succeeding where others of his profession had failed, and his deep sympathy with the victims of the unspeakable cruelty, inspired him to do everything in his power to right one of the most diabolical wrongs to which society has been forced to submit in these later days.

It may be said that the greatest difficulty of all confronted the detective when he had thus located the miscreants. The letters which they sent at intervals to the afflicted family were accompanied by terrifying threats and the demand for an increase of the ransom rose until it reached the stupendous total of fifty thousand dollars. To prevent the criminals from carrying out their threats of vengeance, cunning attempts were made to convince them that the father was doing all he could to comply with their terms. The difficulty of transferring so large a sum made the delay seem reasonable if not unavoidable. In one instance, a large package of genuine bills was placed where directed, but unfortunately for the success of the scheme two carefully disguised detectives were hidden in the vicinity. They were certain they had managed the affair so skilfully that they were not suspected, but the claimants did not go forward and a day later a letter reached Mr. Hastings telling him the trick had been detected and one more repetition of anything of that nature would close all dealings between them, with the certainty that they would never see their child again. A last chance was offered him. He was to place the money in large unmarked bills inside of a traveling bag and throw it off from the rear of the midnight train on a date named, two miles west of Chesterton, at a point indicated so clearly by a pile of towering rocks that no mistake could be made. A failure to comply with this proposal would end all dealings between the kidnappers and the parent.

The night fixed upon was the one succeeding the talk which Detective Pendar held with Harvey Hamilton as related in the preceding chapter. Thus the crisis was at hand,—so near indeed that Pendar had with him the bag and its enormously valuable contents, prepared to carry out, if it could not be avoided, the plan of the miscreants. He had promised that if success was not reached by him before the hour set, he would throw off the money at the point named. Mr. Hastings assured him that if he did not make such a pledge, he himself would do so. He could not suffer the torture any longer, and his wife was already at death's door under the pressure of the grief that was crushing her to the dust.

These frightful letters were mailed from different points, the first reaching the family from a substation in Philadelphia. The last was postmarked at Chesterton, as if the senders wished it to be known they were near the spot where the deal was to be consummated.

A test of Detective Pendar's acumen came in the same hour that he reached the town on the train. At the hotel he quickly fixed upon the two Italians who were registered under the names of Amasi Catozzi and Giuseppe Caprioni, and who spent most of their time in smoking cigarettes and lounging in the sitting-room or on the front porch. Pendar, as has been stated, assumed the character of a commercial traveler for a hardware house, and with no unnecessary delay entered energetically upon his duties. Like a true artist he did not over-do his part, and it is no small proof of his ability to say that he succeeded where almost any other one would have failed. The alert Italians agreed that he was what he represented himself to be, though they by no means relaxed their vigilance.

A point had been reached in the delicate business where a mistake was certain to be fatal. The detective must succeed or fail disastrously. Convinced that the child was held at some point in the adjoining forest, she must be rescued, if rescued at all, by a rush,—a charge, as might be said, that would scatter the wretches in such headlong flight as to compel them to abandon their little prisoner, whom they would not be likely to harm, since their own peril would be increased thereby.

It will be seen, however, that to carry out this coup, the officer must know the exact spot to assail. He could not spend hours in groping through the wood in search of the place, with the certain result that the abductors would take alarm and carry their captive to a secure refuge.

Such was the situation when the arrival of Harvey Hamilton in his aeroplane gave an unexpected turn to affairs. The plan of an aerial hunt for the kidnappers had never occurred to the detective until it forced itself upon him. Here was the means thrust into his hands, and it has been shown how he turned it to account, or, more properly, how he tried to turn it to account, for its success was alarmingly problematical.

The bag with its treasure was deposited in the big safe at the hotel, no one suspecting its contents. Before this time Pendar had reached the pleasing certainty that the two Italians felt no suspicion of him. When he strolled down the long, broad street, smoking a cigar, and now and then halting to look into the store windows, neither of the men shadowed him, as they had done earlier in his visit to Chesterton. The couple were warranted in believing that since Mr. Pendar was all he claimed to be and there were no other suspicious characters in town, they had nothing to fear, the game was still their own.

Thus matters stood when the detective reached the end of the street, and still leisurely walking, passed into the open country. It will be remembered that the moon was near its full and the sky was still unclouded. It was all-important at this point that the kidnappers should not have their attention drawn to him. A scrutiny of the road to the rear removed all doubt on that point.

"It was a pretty hard job," he reflected, "but I have thrown them off the scent and that's a big thing at this stage of the game."

He had passed over the road several times in a carriage on business trips to nearby towns, and was familiar with the forest as viewed from the highway. He knew the precise spot where a path turned in among the trees, which presumably led to the cabin where Bohunkus Johnson had seen the little girl.

Under the shadow of the foliage at the roadside, Pendar stood for fifteen minutes scrutinizing every point in his field of vision. His heart gave a quicker throb when, while looking in the opposite direction from the town, he discerned the dim outlines of a man coming toward him. Pendar whisked back among the shadows, where he could not be seen by the individual approaching.

Whether he was Catozzi or Caprioni remained to be learned. If either of them, the meaning was sinister. From his concealment the watcher observed that the stranger was smoking a pipe. Moreover, he was bulky of frame, stooped with age and had a slouching gait. All this might have been assumed by a young man, but he would fling aside such disguises when believing he was under the eye of no one.

The man passed within ten feet of where Pendar stood behind the trunk of a maple, and in the vivid moonlight the watcher plainly saw the other's profile. The snub nose and retreating chin could not belong to either of the Italians, and this being the fact, the detective had no cause to give the stranger further thought.

The point at which Pendar had stopped was where the path turned into the wood. As nearly as he could judge from the account of Harvey Hamilton, he had about a mile to walk in order to reach the headquarters of the kidnappers, though if the path were winding in its course the distance might be greater. He set out without delay.

It being the summer time, the foliage excluded most of the moonlight and his journey was mainly in darkness, relieved at intervals by spaces where the moonbeams partly penetrated. Even with such occasional help, his progress would have been difficult had he not possessed the skill of an American Indian in threading his way through a trackless forest. No one was ever gifted with keener eyesight or hearing, and he used the two senses to the utmost. He was liable to meet a stranger or to be shadowed by someone. Thus the front and rear had to be guarded. Above all things, he must avoid being discovered while traversing the path, where for most of the way he had to depend upon his sense of feeling. No stronger proof of his subtle woodcraft could be asked than the fact that he never once strayed from his course. He could not have advanced more smoothly had the sun been shining.

While doing this it was his practice to stop at intervals and listen. He reasoned that if some one was approaching from the front, he would not use the extreme caution of an enemy who was following him, for the latter would know of his presence, while an individual coming toward him would not.

The detective had traversed one-half the distance, when in the moonlight he saw a small stream, not more than a rivulet in fact, which wound across the path from the trees on the left and disappeared among those on the right. It was at the bottom of a slight declivity, where a small area was shown in the moonlight. He reflected that if anyone was near, he would see him as he crossed the illuminated space. This could be averted by turning into the wood on either hand, but listening revealed nothing except the faint rustling of the night breeze among the branches. With little hesitation, therefore, he leaped lightly across, hurried up the gentle slope and plunged into the gloom on the other side.

He had gone less than a dozen rods when he abruptly paused, turned his head and listened intently. A minute or two were enough.

"Someone is following me," was his conclusion.

CHAPTER XXV.
A FALSE CLUE.

Detective Pendar instantly whisked out of the path, among the undergrowth and under the trees, where he was invisible to one a foot away. He had heard a faint footfall and the sound was repeated more distinctly when some one leaped across the rivulet and came up the gentle declivity. The officer had gone beyond sight of this open space and the point where the stranger must pass him was shrouded in darkness.

The watcher would have willed it otherwise, for it was important that he should gain a glimpse of the other, but time did not permit, since Pendar could not know how far he would have to hurry over the trail in order to reach such a favorable spot. The trunk of the tree beside which he stood was no more motionless than he. The straining vision saw nothing, but the keen sense of hearing located the stranger as clearly as if at high noon. He passed by like one who had no thought of hiding his progress and the soft footsteps speedily died out.

Before they did so, the officer was back in the path and stealing after him. Fear of detection caused the detective to linger farther in the rear than he wished, but if he erred at all, it was wise that it should be on the side of prudence. Because of the fact named, Pendar lost several chances of getting a sight of the man. The pursuer had decided to wait until the cabin was reached.

That was sooner than he expected, for when he thought he was a considerable way from it he came upon the clearing which had been described to him by Harvey Hamilton. One annoying part of the discovery was that he had lingered too long, for the individual passed through the door in the same moment that Pendar recognized his location. That which he saw told nothing of the form that crossed the threshold and was hidden by the closing of the door.

"Well, here I am," was the thought of our friend, "and I must decide what to do next."

It might have occurred to any one in his situation, that, inasmuch as he had definitely located the kidnappers, he should hasten back to

Chesterton, summon several plucky men whom he had mentally selected two days before, and rush the place, showing scant mercy to the two Italians in town if they ventured to interfere.

But had he discovered the headquarters of the gang?

This question Simmons Pendar asked himself while standing on the edge of the clearing, and staring at the faintly outlined cabin on the other side. Although scarcely a shadow of doubt remained, he felt that that shadow must be removed. He would make further investigation before returning to the hotel.

It was comparatively early in the evening. There were not enough moon-rays to show the face of his watch, but it could not be ten o'clock. A light was burning within the structure, whose interior was hidden by a curtain drawn across each of the two windows,—one on either side of the door. All was silent, and the peering eyes detected no sign of life on the outside.

It was not to be supposed that the abductors of little Grace Hastings would maintain a guard at the cabin itself. Their pickets were at a distance, and unless they gave timely notice of the approach of danger, it would be fatal to the plans of the criminals.

"I wonder whether they keep a dog," was the thought which held the watcher motionless for a little while; "if they do, he'll play the mischief with me."

Could he have been assured that a canine was on watch, the detective would not have dared to go a step nearer the dwelling, but would have made all haste to Chesterton and arranged for his raid, since discovery at this stage of the game would be the end of hope.

"It strikes me that if they have a dog on guard, he ought to have discovered me by this time—Thunderation! there he comes now!"

A canine as large as a wolf came trotting across the clearing, heading directly for Simmons Pendar. It was useless to run, for the terrible brute would have been at his heels in an instant. He laid his hand on his revolver.

"If he attacks, I'll shoot him and then the fat will be in the fire."

While the dog was several paces away and after Pendar had drawn his weapon from his hip pocket, he spoke in soothing tones to him. The animal did not bark or growl, but seemed to be pleased by his friendly greeting. He came on, and the man never used his persuasive powers more skilfully. He called him all the pet names he could think of, and when the brute was within reach, reached out and patted his head.

To his pleased astonishment, he completely won the good will of the dog, which wagged his bushy tail so energetically that it swayed his haunches. He whined, snuffed about the man's knees, and then abruptly raised one of his big paws, which the eavesdropper was instant to seize and shake.

"Bully for you!" exclaimed Pendar in a guarded voice; "I don't know that your owner would be pleased with your performance, but I'm mighty sure I am."

He petted him a few minutes longer, when the canine turned about and trotted back to the house. There he scratched upon the door and whined until it was opened from within and he passed out of sight.

"Considered from my point of view," said the detective grimly, "that dog is a model guardian of a house, but those who expect vigilance from him probably hold a different opinion."

Nothing could be gained by remaining where he was, for all he could see was the shadowy outline of a tumble-down log cabin and a few scattered outbuildings. It was necessary to gain a look at the interior. The cheap faded curtains at the front windows shut out any view, but he was hopeful of success from the rear. He made a careful circuit of the building, keeping at a goodly distance until he reached a point opposite to that which he had first held. Then he began stealing forward. Before doing so, he noticed that neither of the rear windows possessed anything in the nature of a curtain. He had only to come close to them to see everything in the room where the light was burning.

Now that the dog was out of the way, even with his friendly disposition, the detective felt no apprehension, unless there might be some one on guard—a thing improbable—or a member of the company should draw near from the direction followed by himself.

The yellow rays of a tallow candle, aided by the moonlight, which had partial sway on this side of the cabin, made the task easy for Pendar. He crept steadily forward until under one of the windows, when he rose to his feet, just far enough to peer over the sill. Even before doing so, he was troubled by a misgiving. Something in all this experience was out of keeping with the character of a band of kidnappers.

The detective's position could not have been more favorable, for the face of no one was turned toward the window, where he might have been discovered. What he saw was this:

Evidently the evening meal had been kept waiting to so late an hour in order to accommodate the last arrival, who was an old man, seated at the head of a plain deal table without cover, and with only several of the plainest dishes of food. Opposite at the farther end, sat the wife, a bulky, gray-haired, slatternly woman, presiding over the teapot and a few of the minor articles of food. The huge dog was sleeping on the floor near the hearth. On the side of the table, with her back toward the wall, sat a little girl, probably five or six years old, eating from a bowl of bread and milk. She was continually chattering, so that her profile was often shown to Pendar, whose heart sank within him upon the first good look at her features.

She was not Grace Hastings. The detective carried a cabinet picture of the stolen child with whose face he was as familiar as with that of his own child. It showed a chubby, comely little girl, with abundant curly hair, almost black. The one before him had straight, scant yellow hair and her face was thin, as if from recent illness. It would be hard to picture two children of tender years so different in appearance.

Something in the looks of the head of the family was familiar, and it took the officer but a few moments to identify him. You will recall Uncle Tommy, the famous local prophet, who told Harvey Hamilton what kind of weather to expect, when he descended at Chesterton. The man was Uncle Tommy and the others were his wife and child, or possibly a grandchild.

Detective Pendar gave utterance to a forceful exclamation, for he was filled with rage and chagrin. He would have made affidavit a few minutes before, and at any time after his talk with the young aviator, that he had located the headquarters of the gang of kidnappers, with the recovery of the stolen child only a question of a few hours.

He had failed utterly. He had reconnoitered the home of a plain, simple-minded inhabitant, who lived in poverty in this cabin, and was as innocent of stealing a child as Harvey Hamilton himself.

A faint hope held Pendar where he was for a brief while longer. It might be that the abductors had made their home in this cabin, whose owner and wife were under their domination and employ. But brief reflection showed the officer that no supposition could be more preposterous. He backed from the window, careless now whether discovered or not, threaded his course to the trail over which he had come with so much care, and started on his return to Chesterton.

"Josh Billings once said it is so easy for a man to be a fool that he can do so without knowing it. The difference in my case is that I know it; I'm mighty glad that none of the boys will ever hear of it."

Bitter as were his reflections they brightened as he strode over the trail, to the highway leading to the hotel. Something like hope returned to him.

"I have reason to believe that the gang is somewhere in that big stretch of woods. Young Hamilton mistook the building, which can't be far off. I have learned enough to be sure on that point."

But there was no escaping the terrifying truth that the time which remained for him to work out any scheme he might formulate was reduced to hours instead of days. If by midnight of the next day he was still confronted by failure, he was pledged to board the westward bound train with his bag containing fifty thousand dollars, and to throw it off at a point that had been so clearly described that there could be no mistaking it.

"It looks as if that is all that's left," he muttered in the bitterness of spirit, "it's an infernal shame, but I see little hope of any other issue."

CHAPTER XXVI.
THE SEARCH RENEWED.

Harvey Hamilton was in the middle of an odd dream, in which a big Irishman was swinging a tremendous hammer and bringing it down on the top of his head with every stroke. The sentiment of wonder is always absent in the visions which come to us in sleep, no matter how incongruous they may be, but the youth came very near feeling surprised at the thickness of a skull that could withstand so terrific attacks.

By and by the slumber lifted and Harvey's senses came back. He was wide awake and conscious that some one was tapping gently outside. He sprang out of bed and turned the key. As if automatically, the door swung inward and revealed Detective Pendar in the dim gaslight. He stepped within and secured the lock behind him.

"Sh!" he whispered; "I don't think either of those men is in his room, but we cannot be too careful."

The night was so sultry that Harvey did not dress, but sat down on the edge of the bed, his caller doing the same, near enough to be touched with the outstretched hand. The time had come for the officer to tell more than was his rule in circumstances of a critical nature.

"How did you succeed?" asked the younger.

"It's a fizzle so far," was the reply; "I have inspected that cabin in the woods, where you and I thought the little girl was held a prisoner, but she is not there now and never has been there."

And then he told his story to the astonished and disappointed listener.

"Understand, no blame attaches to you," the detective hastened to add; "your mistake was natural and I could have made it as readily as you."

This was not strictly true. The picture which Bunk Johnson viewed from the biplane would have been analyzed to the point of disclosing the truth, had Pendar been the one who saw it.

"Then I suppose, you will give up the hunt?"

"By no means, but it must end one way or another before we are twenty-four hours older."

This assertion opened the way for the startling revelation that if Grace Hastings was not recovered before the ensuing midnight, the ransom would be paid by the officer, who had it waiting in the safe of the hotel below stairs.

"Although you mistook the place where the gang are holding her," added the man, "you came near it. Did either you or your colored friend notice any other house in the woods when you were sailing over them?"

"I gave my attention to the management of the aeroplane after observing the cabin, and could easily have passed several dwellings without seeing them. Bunk spoke of no other, though it is possible he saw one."

"I have information which cannot be questioned that the spot we are looking for is not far from the home of Uncle Tommy Waters the weather prophet. Had my investigation been made by daylight, I should have pushed it farther, but I was helpless at night. You will have to make another search as soon as it is daylight."

"I am eager to do what I can, but you must tell me how."

"Is your negro capable of running your aeroplane?"

"He can when the conditions are favorable, as they promise to be to-morrow; I shouldn't be willing to trust him otherwise."

"Good! let him handle the levers then, while you occupy the aluminum chair and give your efforts to spying out the land."

"Shall we follow the same course as before?"

"Substantially so; he will keep the speed just high enough to sustain you at an altitude of say five hundred feet. You understand that the closer you are to the ground, the narrower is your field of vision, so you will keep far enough aloft to gain an extended survey, and yet not so high that you will lose distinctness of view. I notice that you carry a field glass."

"Yes; it is of German make and the best in the world; our government sells them only to its army and navy officers; mine belongs to one who is a relative, and who has loaned the instrument to me for life, I making a suitable money acknowledgment therefor."

This pleasant little fictional arrangement explains how it is that some of these fine instruments are in the hands of civilians.

"You are not likely to need the glasses on this trip."

"Hardly; the heights from which I am to make the search are so moderate that my eyes will require no help."

"Then will you loan them to me?"

"With pleasure."

The detective explained the use to which he expected to put the binoculars.

"I shall take a position that will give me an extended survey over the woods without drawing notice to myself, and after you are fairly started on your aerial voyage, I do not intend to lose sight of you."

"If I discover the place you have in mind, how shall I let you know it?"

"By signal."

"They will be likely to see it."

"Not likely but certain; therefore the message must be of a nature that will not rouse suspicion on their part."

Harvey could not forbear asking an explanation at this point.

"You said that if your visit to the cabin had been made by daylight, you would have gone farther. Why not do so in the morning?"

"I should if time permitted. You understand that without your aid I should have to make a hunt through the woods. This would not only consume time but would surely be discovered by some of the gang on the lookout. That is why I have refrained and waited for an opportunity to present itself. When you locate the exact spot—and I am sure you will do so—I can go straight to it."

"Will you not be watched?"

"Quite likely, but I can push on in spite of that. Let us get back to the important point of how you are to let me know of your success. The simplest thing is—I'm blessed if I know," said the detective, after slight hesitation, with a laugh; "help me out."

That which at first seemed an insignificant matter threatened to become insurmountable. Pendar's first suggestion was that when Harvey made his discovery he should swing his cap over his head, but such a signal would be instantly noticed by the kidnappers, who would accept it as a menace.

"Suppose I tell Bunk to swoop downward as if about to make a landing."

"That would be fully as bad, for the scoundrels would think it was meant to gain a clearer view of them."

"If we sail upward?"

"That's it! They can give no meaning to such a manœuver. When you are sure of what you see, direct your servant to go upward at the sharpest angle possible. I shall be the only one who will know what the movement means."

"It seems to me," added the youth thoughtfully, "that those two Italians who are stopping at the hotel must begin to suspect you."

"Not as yet; I count myself fortunate that I have thrown them off the scent completely. There is no doubt of that, though it looks as if there will be a waking up before to-morrow night."

"You have played your part with skill, Mr. Pendar."

"I'll not deny that I feel some pride over my work thus far; but, all the same, I have as yet accomplished nothing, and it is by no means certain that I shall do anything more than pay a set of criminals fifty thousand dollars to give back the child they have stolen."

At this point Harvey recalled the other matters that had slipped his mind during his previous talk with the detective.

"You know, Mr. Pendar, that since Bunk and I started on our little sail through the upper regions, we have several times run across a curious character called Professor Milo Morgan."

"I know him well; he is a crank of the first order."

"He was friendly at first and did me a great favor when I was in danger of being mobbed, but it is hard to forgive one of his acts."

"What was that?"

"Wrecking my aeroplane, by chopping and battering it to pieces when it was housed under the sheds of this hotel."

The detective rose from the side of the bed and stood upright in the gloom in front of his young friend.

"What in the name of the seven wonders put that fancy into your head?"

"Why," replied Harvey hesitatingly, not expecting such an implied contradiction; "it couldn't have been any one else."

"Well, it was some one else; Professor Morgan had no more to do with destroying your biplane than King George V."

The amazed Harvey stared in astonishment.

"Bunk saw him sneaking out of the back of the shed early in the morning, when he went to look at the machine."

"Did the Professor have an axe or hatchet in his hand?"

"I believe not."

"Having told you what he did not do, can you now form an idea of what he did do?"

"I suppose he went off in that marvelous monoplane of his."

"But previous to that?"

"I haven't the remotest idea."

"He went to the telegraph office as soon as it was open, and sent your father a long message, giving the particulars of your misfortune. Your father, like the good fellow he is, immediately ordered a new machine, which reached you this morning."

"I am amazed and gratified," replied Harvey; "the first chance I have I shall apologize to Professor Morgan."

"Don't do that."

"Why not?"

"He will know that you have been idiot enough to suspect him."

"But, Mr. Pendar, do you know who did destroy my machine?"

"Don't you?"

"I have no suspicion."

"Well, I shall leave you to solve one of the simplest problems that was ever submitted to a ten-year old child. I was so certain you knew the truth at once, that I didn't think it worth while to make any reference to it when we next spoke together."

CHAPTER XXVII.
BOHUNKUS AT THE LEVERS.

Fortunately for Detective Pendar, the room which he occupied at the hotel in Chesterton gave him a view of the immense forest to the westward, over which Harvey Hamilton's aeroplane was to sail in its search for the headquarters of the men who had kidnapped little Grace Hastings.

The keen-witted officer was right in his belief that he had diverted suspicion from himself, but how long this favorable situation would continue was problematical to the last degree. It seemed impossible to make any effective move without betraying his real character, as well as the business that had brought him to this little country town in eastern Pennsylvania.

Pendar easily learned one fact: neither Catozzi nor Caprioni had occupied their room the previous night, nor did they show up in the morning at the hotel. His theory was that the couple had gone to the retreat in the woods, where they were likely to stay until the ransom was paid for the child. The nearness of the crisis made this reasoning plausible. It followed, therefore, that at the time the detective was threading his way through the gloomy labyrinths, they were doing the same, though over a different course. They and he must have been near each other some time during the night, but it was well he saw nothing of them. While it may be difficult for one person to shadow another in certain circumstances, an Apache warrior could not have trailed two vigilant kidnappers, when they were alert against such a betrayal. The chances would have been in favor of the detective himself being discovered and all his schemes brought to naught.

In his exceeding caution, he continued to meet the two youths as if they were strangers. When the time came for the starting of the aeroplane, Pendar did not join the gaping crowd, but stayed in his room on the upper floor, awaiting the call to use his field glass. He heard the deafening roar of the motor, and a minute later saw the odd looking structure climb from the open space into the upper regions, and sail away to the westward. He saw Bohunkus Johnson, the proudest youth in the whole country, seated in front, with his hands upon the levers, behind him was Harvey Hamilton with a sharp eye upon his movements.

Detective Pendar saw the aeroplane slant upward and travel at a rapid pace. It was not necessary to employ his glasses, and he watched the flight of the machine until it was nearly a half mile away. Then he brought the instrument to his eyes, carefully adjusted the focal distance and did not allow anything to escape his searching vision. His first sensation was pleased surprise over the excellence of the instrument. Every outline of the aeroplane came out clear and sharp, and it seemed as if the two youths were near enough for them to hear him if he spoke in a conversational tone. He noticed that the negro continued to sit straight, as if under the eyes of the crowd that had seen him leave Chesterton, but Harvey Hamilton was leaning slightly forward, like one studying every feature of the landscape sweeping under him.

The several days which the detective had spent in the neighborhood had given him a good knowledge of its topography. He was quick, therefore, to observe that the aeroplane was following a course well to the north of its former one. This was prudent on the part of the young aviator, for it gave him new view instead of the old one which could serve him no further. He was approaching the ridge over which he had sailed the previous day.

As the distance between the watcher and the aeroplane rapidly increased, the detective almost held his breath. He was leaning against the window sill in order to make his posture firm and prevent the slightest wavering of the instrument. With one hand he occasionally turned the little cogged wheel in front so as to keep the focus right, and not allow the slightest detail to escape him.

"He is as far to the west as Uncle Tommy's house, but a half mile north of that. This will show him all he needs to see in that direction."

The watcher's heart began to misgive him, for the machine was fast receding, and though Harvey must be intently watching he failed to make any sign. Even with the power of the field glass, the great bird with its spreading wings began to flicker, and Pendar was no longer able to clearly make out the forms of the youths seated therein.

Suddenly the aeroplane flickered, became indistinct and the nearer margin of the woods shut it from sight.

"Another failure!" muttered the watcher bitterly. "I may as well get ready to hand over that fortune to as vile a gang as was ever disgorged from the mountains of Sicily."

The upper sash was lowered that he might obtain an unobstructed view of the soft tinted sky beyond. He took care to stand far enough back in the room to be out of sight of any persons in the street below. If either of the Italians had returned, he did not mean they should learn how he was spending the minutes.

"I did not provide last night what young Hamilton should do if he failed to make the discovery on his first, or rather second voyage over the woods. It will be risky for him to come back, but it may look as if he were on a little trial trip with his negro and wished to return so as to take charge himself. If he does that he will take a course to the south of his first trip, and, by Jove! there he comes!"

It gave the detective an expectant thrill to see the ship of the sky swim into his field of vision and head directly toward him. Harvey Hamilton was following the plan which had presented itself to the man. The first flight disclosed the home of Uncle Tommy Waters the weather prophet; the second revealed nothing, and the third, well to the south, must tell the tale. The crisis was at hand.

The officer did not call his field glass into play. The aeroplane was not only plainly visible, but was becoming more vivid every minute. Its elevation was five or six hundred feet, and the watcher breathlessly waited for the sudden shift that was to proclaim the discovery. The machine skimmed through the air without deviation, like a stone when it first leaves the sling, and then the abrupt shift came.

But to Pendar's consternation the aeroplane instead of shooting upward dived toward the ground!

He snatched the glasses to his eyes. By their aid he saw Harvey Hamilton leaning forward and gesticulating excitedly to Bohunkus

Johnson. The deafening racket of the engine rendered his voice useless, but he managed to make his wishes known. In desperate need he might reach the levers, and if anything had gone wrong with the machine this would have been done. But it was quickly evident that there had been a misunderstanding between the two. Bohunkus must have thought Harvey meant him to approach the earth, though it was impossible to land unless some open space presented itself. The dipping of the forward rudder brought the biplane half way down before the controller comprehended what was expected of him. Then he pointed the horizontal plane upward at so great an angle that the ascent became startlingly rapid.

Even in the extremity of anxiety, Detective Pendar could not repress a smile at the sight which the glass revealed. The head of Bunk kept flitting back and forth, in his efforts to handle the machine and to learn what Harvey was trying to tell him. Pendar saw the young aviator shake his fist angrily, and once he seemed on the point of cuffing the heavy-witted youth for his stupidity. For a minute or two the aeroplane wavered and swayed to that degree that it seemed on the point of capsizing, but Bohunkus gradually regained control, and began his manœuvers to land in the open space from which he had ascended. He made a mess of it, the wheels striking the ground so hard that both the boys came within a hair of pitching out. Then the biplane banged over the road, coming to a halt barely in time to escape a disastrous collision with a telegraph pole.

"The next time you want to try your hand," said the angry Harvey, "I'll put you in charge of a clam wagon."

Bohunkus Johnson and Harvey Hamilton having been playmates from young childhood, had indulged in the usual number of "spats" natural to such a relation. They were fond of each other and the colored youth as a rule accepted the criticisms of his friend with good nature; but in the present instance the reproof given him was made in the presence of fully a score of men and boys and was heard by all of them. Several grinned, and had not nature made it impossible, Bunk would have flushed with resentment. As it was, he could not accept the slur with meekness.

"I done as well as yo' could yo'self. Yo' told me of I seed a cabin I was to shoot down and knock de chimbly off, and den when I started to do so, yo' let out a howl dat nearly knocked my cap off. De next time yo' can 'tend to things yo'self."

"You may be mighty sure I shall; the wonder is that you didn't smash this machine worse than the other one."

"I wouldn't keer if I did," replied Bunk, stepping from his seat and striding off. He paused long enough to call back:

"I'm done trabeling wid yo'; I like to hab folks 'preciate what's done for 'em, which is what yo' never did."

"The best thing you can do, Bunk, is to sail for Africa and make a visit to Chief Foozleum."

Harvey laughed when he made this remark, for he never could feel angry for more than a few minutes with the faithful fellow, and he knew his resentment would soon cool. It did not occur to him that the colored youth's grievance was due to the tantalizing enjoyment of the auditors. Had they been elsewhere, he would have brushed the criticism aside like so much thistle down, but he could not stand the ridicule of strangers.

"Dat's what I'll do," replied Bunk in response to the absurd counsel of the other.

"All right; bring me back an elephant."

Bunk had learned that in a verbal duel with Harvey he was always sure to get the worst of it, and he did not venture any reply to the last remark. With an angry sniff he stalked to the porch, dropped into one of the chairs there, crossed his legs and scowlingly watched the actions of his old friend.

Little did Harvey Hamilton dream what the result would be of this brief and somewhat hot exchange of words.

Convinced that the angry fellow would speedily regain his natural good humor, Harvey gave him no further thought. He made a careful examination of his aeroplane, and was relieved to find, so far as he could discover, that it had suffered no harm and was as good as ever.

He was anxious now to meet Detective Pendar, for he had important news for him, but the man was nowhere in sight nor could the youth tell where to look for him.

CHAPTER XXVIII.
FIRED ON BY THE KIDNAPPERS.

When glancing around in quest of Detective Pendar, Harvey Hamilton failed to look behind him. Some one touched his shoulder, as he stood beside his aeroplane. Glancing back, there was his man.

The time for them to be strangers to each other had passed. Pendar asked crisply:

"How did you make out?"

"I found the spot."

"Certain there is no mistake about it?"

"I saw the little girl herself; we have located her."

"Can you take me thither?"

"Yes, but I can't land; there isn't enough space."

"Let me down in front of Uncle Tommy's home; it isn't far off."

"All right; take your seat; I'll have you there in a jiffy. I didn't see either of those men."

"There's one of them now on the edge of the crowd, toward the porch of the hotel."

While the detective was seating himself, the young aviator looked in the direction indicated. The Italian, Amasi Catozzi, was standing a little apart from the others, watching the couple as a cat watches a mouse which she expects to come within reach of her claws the next moment. Dressed in a gray, natty suit and slouch hat, he kept his hands in the pockets of his coat, which was buttoned to his gaudy necktie.

The hurried words between the man and boy must have told the truth to the Black Hander. The individual whom he had accepted as a commercial traveler was a professional detective, whose search for the kidnapped child had brought him to this country town and very near the spot where she was held a prisoner. He must have believed, too, that the aeroplane had come thither, not accidentally, but to play an assigned part in the drama. The prospect of the whole daring scheme being brought to naught filled the miscreant with unrestrainable rage. He stood for a moment like a statue, his swarthy face aflame with passion. Then he took several hasty steps forward as if to interfere. The propeller of the biplane was revolving faster and faster, and it began gliding down the moderate slope, preparatory to leaping upward from the earth. Harvey, with hands and feet busy, gave his whole attention to the task, but the shrewd Pendar rightly suspected they were not yet through with the wretch who strode toward them.

The machine was in the act of leaving the ground when Catozzi's right hand was jerked out of his coat pocket. Leveling a revolver, he blazed away twice in rapid succession at the detective. The latter had turned in his seat so as to face him, and was barely a second behind him in returning the shot.

The couple were not fifty feet apart when this interchange took place. The Italian was an expert with firearms and had he not been incited by so consuming a passion, he assuredly would have got his man. He missed by a hair's breadth, but the cool Simmons Pendar did better. He saw his enemy's body twitch, the Italian staggered backward a couple of paces, and the pistol dropped from his grasp.

The detective knew, however, that he had only winged him. In truth he had not tried to kill but only to wound, and he succeeded. In that moment Pendar, who generally held himself well in hand, felt such a thrill of anger that he determined to end the wretch's power for evil forever. He sighted his weapon with the utmost care, and had the conditions been favorable, he assuredly would have scored a "bull's eye," but it must be remembered that the aeroplane was in action, and already in the air, heading westward and going at a speed of thirty or forty miles an hour.

Moreover, Bohunkus Johnson at this point got into the game. He had seated himself, as we remember, on the porch and was sulking over the reproof of Harvey Hamilton. Now when he saw him going off without him, he sprang to his feet; leaped down the few steps, dashed forward and shouted:

"Hold on, Harv! Yo've forgot something!"

But his friend could not wait for him. In the racket made by the motor, he heard nothing, and, if he had caught the words he would have paid no heed. Far more weighty matters claimed his undivided efforts. The action of the colored youth, however, brought him in direct line with the Italian, and the fast receding detective dared not fire because of the danger of hitting the negro or some member of the group of staring spectators.

The incidents described took so brief a time that no one who witnessed them understood what had taken place until all was ended. Certainly they could not have dreamed of its meaning. Why the drummer seated behind the young aviator should turn about and exchange shots with another man who seemed also to be a drummer, was more than any person could figure out, unless he laid it to bitter business rivalry.

Conversation between Harvey Hamilton and Detective Pendar was impossible, nor was it necessary. The few sentences spoken were sufficient, though had there been the opportunity, the man would have asked for more particulars. Although on this warm summer day he wore no top coat, he carried two pairs of patent handcuffs, and his weapon still held four charges, which no man in the world better knew how to utilize. He would have been very glad to stand up in front of the raging Catozzi with both their revolvers cracking and only a few paces between them, but the time had not yet come for a duel of that kind. He gave his intensest attention to what was before him while Harvey Hamilton was equally resolute with his duty.

Catozzi was not hit so hard as he thought when the twinge first thrilled his shoulder. The bullet of the detective inflicted only a flesh wound, and the man rallied instantly from the shock. He recovered his weapon and for a minute watched the aeroplane speeding away like an enormous bird. Then he noted that its line of flight was directly over the spot. Not a vestige of doubt remained as to what this meant.

The landlord had come out on the porch during the stirring incidents and now approached the Italian.

"What the mischief did that man mean by shooting at you? Did he hurt you bad?"

"No, no, no," replied Catozzi, who despite the fact that a crimson stain was beginning to show on his upper arm angrily added:

"I am not hurt; don't bother me."

He set off down the street, taking the direction followed by the detective the night before. He walked fast until he reached the beginning of the path which led to the home of the ancient weather prophet. There he turned off and his pace became almost a run. He needed no one to tell him the desperate need of haste.

He had gone only half way when he left the main path and followed a faintly marked trail,—so dimly indicated indeed that any person not keen sighted or looking for something of the kind would have missed it altogether.

Meanwhile Harvey Hamilton was attending strictly to business. Directly south of the tumble-down home of Uncle Tommy Waters, and less than an eighth of a mile away, stood a smaller and more dilapidated cabin, with no signs of cultivation about it. It seemed wedged among a mass of rocks and stones, which formed a part of the structure. One side was wholly composed of rocks. Surveying the miserable shanty, one would have concluded that it had never been used as a permanent dwelling, but might have been flung into shape by a party of hunters who, visiting that section, had aimed to provide against sudden storm and preferred to sleep there rather than at any house or in the town.

When the aeroplane was skimming over this unattractive spot, Harvey turned his head and, meeting the glance of the detective, nodded. The gesture said: "That's the place," and the answering nod indicated that the man understood.

What it was that had told the young aviator the startling truth was more than his companion could guess, for, search as he might, he could not detect the first sign of life below them. There was the gray pile of boards and rails, which looked as if they had been tossed among the boulders by a cyclone, but nothing else met the eye. All the same, the youth had not been mistaken.

Had not the interest of the two been centered upon what was beneath them, they would have made an interesting discovery. Less than a mile distant, a monoplane, as close to the earth as their own, was bearing down upon them. One glance would have made known to our friends that it was the well remembered Dragon of the Skies. There could be no doubt that its owner, Professor Milo Morgan, was on his way to take part in the game. But that interesting fact was not learned until a brief while later.

Having shown his companion the cabin he had sought so long, Harvey Hamilton shot beyond it, and circled about until over the clearing in front of Uncle Tommy Waters' home, when he began descending by means of the spiral, that picturesque and graceful manœuver, always attended with peril, as was shown on the last day of the year 1910, when the daring aviator Arch Hoxsey was killed at Los Angeles and John B. Moisant met his death at New Orleans.

It will be remembered that the biplane was at an elevation of not more than five hundred feet when he began to volplane. The forenoon was clear, and radiant with sunshine. There was no breeze except that which was caused by the motion of the aeroplane. Harvey had excellent control, and was confident of coming down at the spot selected, when, without the slightest warning, he was caught in the fierce grip of an eddy, whirlpool or pocket, or whatever it might be called, and tossed about as if he were a feather. The ailerons fluttered and the machine lurched like a mortally wounded bird, frantically trying to hold its place in the air. Recalling the instructions of Professor Sperbeck, Harvey did not run away from the startling flurry, but plunged straight into it. It was another illustration of the peril to which all aviators are exposed, of being caught at any unexpected moment by the currents that must always be invisible.

Harvey braced himself, hoping that a few seconds would carry him across the zone of danger, and came within a hair of pitching from his seat. The wabbling machine suddenly tilted upward, and stood almost vertical. The escape of Detective Pendar was equally narrow. Although he gripped the supports with both hands, it seemed to him that for one terrible moment he hung by them alone, with his legs dangling in midair. He was certain the aeroplane was capsizing, and he could only wait for the end of all things. Gladly would he have given the whole reward, which dazzled his vision, for the privilege of feeling the solid earth under his feet.

CHAPTER XXIX.
RETRIBUTION.

Their frightful peril lasted only a few seconds. Although the machine still swayed like a ship laboring among surges, it struck more tranquil air, and with its graceful spiral motion lightly touched the ground, ran to the edge of the clearing and stopped with its front rigger within a few feet of a huge oak on the edge of the open space.

It was still spinning forward when Detective Pendar leaped from his seat, and without a word to Harvey Hamilton, who, of course, had shut off the motor, dashed away on a run through the wood, making for the spot among the rocks where the pile of lumber and rails disclosed the headquarters of the kidnapping gang. He had not yet seen one of them, but knew they whom he sought were there.

Before he reached the spot he caught sight through the treetops of the monoplane of Professor Morgan heading for the same point. Recognizing him he uttered an impatient exclamation.

"He's going to mix in and spoil everything."

As easily and noiselessly as a soaring eagle, the circling machine came to a rest directly over the ramshackle structure. The wonderful "uplifter" was spinning under the monoplane and held it motionless over the exact spot, at a height of barely a hundred feet.

Detective Pendar in a frenzy of excitement leaped into the scant open space, where he was in sight of the aviator, who, as he had done in a former instance, stood erect, with a large oblong object in his hand to which he was about to apply a lighted match. Reading his purpose, Pendar shouted:

"Don't do that! You'll kill the little girl!"

Professor Morgan did not seem to hear him, or, if he did, paid no attention.

"Don't, Professor! You will kill the child!"

The man now called down from his elevation:

"Don't be alarmed! She is not there!"

"I know she is," insisted Pendar, drawing his revolver. "If you drop that bomb I'll shoot you!"

The tall, ungainly figure remained upright. He had lighted the fuse which was spitting flame. He still held it in his hand and was carefully sighting with the purpose of making it fall where he wished.

"I tell you the girl is not there, but the men are! Put up that pistol or I'll throw the bomb at you and send you to kingdom come with them!"

The naturally cool-headed detective was beside himself. The calm assurance of the crank overhead stayed his hand. He did not know what to do and therefore did nothing.

"Stand back!" warned the aviator; "or you'll catch it too!"

The words were yet in his mouth, when an object eight or ten inches in length, two or three inches in diameter and of a dull gray color, left his hand and dived downward. The fuse was smoking and the bomb turned end over end several times before it alighted on the warped boards which served for a roof to the structure. It lay there for a brief interval, during which it jerked to the right and left, as a spurting hose will do when no one is holding it, then it toppled over and dropped through a gap in the boards.

The next instant there was muffled, thunderous report, and rocks, rails and splintered wood flew in every direction, as if from the mouth of Vesuvius. The bomb had exploded with terrific force, and a noise that stunned the spectator, who caught a glimpse of something resembling a huge bird which darted toward him. A rail, as if fired from a modern siege gun, whizzed within a few inches of his head and skittered among the branches behind him.

THE BOMB HAD EXPLODED WITH TERRIFIC FORCE.

In those terrifying moments the detective saw another sight,—one that held him dumfounded for a brief interval. Among the flying debris was the form of a man, which shot upward for fifty feet, turning over, passed above the head of Pendar and fell among the trees, where it lay still and motionless.

A second man came rolling like a log rushing down hill and settled to rest a few paces in front of the shocked spectator. His clothing was on fire in a dozen places. Rousing himself, the officer snatched off his coat, and hurriedly wrapped it about the wretch, who lay still, moaning with pain.

But in the midst of the fearful scene, Simmons Pendar glanced around in quest of that which he dreaded to see above everything else in the world. Harvey Hamilton had identified the stolen child and how could she escape that awful explosion? But she was not to be seen, and with relief unspeakable he decided that Professor Morgan was truthful in his declaration. Paying no heed for the moment to the man at his feet, the detective looked upward and shouted:

"Where is she?"

There was no reply, for Professor Morgan was not there, or at least was beyond hearing or replying to the question. Having accomplished that which he had in mind to do, he had set his silent machine again in motion, and was fast vanishing in the direction of the town of Chesterton.

Relieved of his great fear, Pendar stooped over the form at his feet. To his amazement the man seemed to have suffered only trifling injuries. The enwrapping of the coat had put out the incipient flames and the fellow came as easily to his feet as if rising from sleep. He said something to the detective in his own language, which was not understood. Pendar reached out and taking his scorched garment quietly put it on himself, but in the act of doing so he gave proof of his professional deftness by slipping a pair of handcuffs on his prisoner before he suspected the trick. He struggled desperately to free himself, and unable to do so, tried to strike his captor with the irons which clasped his wrists. But all that remained possible was to try to run away, and the detective was prepared to defeat an attempt of that nature.

That the fellow understood English became clear the next minute, when Pendar drew his revolver from his hip pocket and addressed him:

"If you try to run off I'll shoot you!"

"Me no run off," replied the man, cowering with fear. Probably his meekness was pretense with a view of gaining an advantage over his captor.

"Where is that little girl you stole from her home in Philadelphia?"

The prisoner shrugged his shoulders and shook his head:

"Me no understand."

"Yes, you do; answer before I fire!"

And the weapon was leveled with the muzzle within a few inches of the man's face, which was contorted by terror.

"Don't know," he hastened to say.

Detective Pendar was enraged enough to shoot him. With a dreadful sinking of hope the officer asked himself whether there was to be a miscarriage of justice after all. Grace Hastings was neither within the shanty nor anywhere near it when Professor Morgan blew it up with his bomb. Could it be that the abductors had discovered their danger before that time and removed the little one to a safe retreat, or could it be——

He dared not finish the question. One thing was clear: the negotiations that had been carried on for so many days were now ended, and could never be renewed. The friends of the child had proved their determination not to pay the ransom demanded, and no more communication could be held between them and the kidnappers.

Humanity seemed to demand that attention should be given to him who was hurled among the trees in the rear by the explosion; but in the intensity of his chagrin and wrath, Detective Pendar decided that, as he was already past help, time would be wasted upon him. Although the garments of the prisoner showed faint wisps of smoke here and there, the fire was gradually dying out and he was in no danger from that cause. His captor compressed his lips with the resolution to force the truth from the wretch. Surely he could throw light upon the disappearance of the child, and the detective was resolute in his purpose of forcing him to do so.

"What is your name?" was the first question of the master of the situation, who, noticing the other's shrug and hesitation, added: "You needn't pretend you don't understand me. What is your name, I repeat?"

"Alessandro Pierotti," was the answer.

"Who was the man that was blown into the wood behind me?"

"Giuseppe Caprioni."

To test the truthfulness of the fellow Detective Pendar now demanded the name of the other member of the group that had loitered during the last few days about the hotel in Chesterton. Pierotti gave it correctly, and his questioner was convinced that all were right.

"That makes three. Who were the others connected with you?"

"No more,—that all."

The detective did not believe this, aware as he was of the fearful penalties that are visited by members of the Black Hand upon those who betray their associates. He wondered in fact why Pierotti had not tried to deceive him as to the names. It may have been because he believed the truth was at the command of this captor. That others were connected with his crime was a certainty, but this was not the time nor place in which to probe the matter.

"How long did you have the little girl in this part of the country?"

The frightened prisoner wrinkled his brow in thought.

"A week,—almost—not quite."

"Where is she now?"

"Went off—she play—she soon come back."

This statement was perplexing and Pendar did not understand it.

"When did she go?"

"One—two—tree hour; she soon come back," he repeated.

"Who went with her?"

"No one—she go with herself; she not go far."

"Which way?"

Pierotti pointed in the direction of the cabin of Uncle Tommy Waters. The path which has been mentioned as dimly marked, took another course before joining the main trail which branched off from the highway a little way out from Chesterton.

While it seemed improbable that a captive like Grace Hastings would have been permitted anything in the nature of freedom at so critical a time, the detective decided to act upon the statement.

"Lead the way, Pierotti; I shall walk behind you; if you try to slip off, or I find you have deceived me, look out!"

CHAPTER XXX.
THE RESCUE.

Harvey Hamilton was anything but pleased over the actions of Detective Pendar in dashing off as he did without a word of explanation. He expected to accompany him, and would have followed but through fear of offending his friend. The youth could not forget that he possessed nothing in the nature of a weapon and was more likely to prove a hindrance rather than a help to the officer.

"He is a brave man,—a reckless one," he reflected, "thus to rush upon a desperate gang who are armed and will stop at no crime. Hello! what does that mean?"

He had stepped down from his seat and glanced over his machine, when chancing to look up in the sky he recognized the monoplane of Professor Morgan, already near the spot where the young aviator had seen the ruined shanty not long before, with the little girl playing in front of it.

The discovery that the odd character had not wrecked his first machine, but had been the means of his securing a second with remarkable promptness, changed the resentment of the youth to the kindliest feelings toward the man. He watched the actions with fascinated interest, for the distance was so slight that everything was visible. It has been said that one of the achievements of Professor Morgan was the knack of running his monoplane with scarcely any perceptible noise. A misty, whirring object under his perch showed that the "uplifter" was doing its effective work and holding the machine motionless over the place desired.

It was far enough for the intervening forest to muffle the voices of the airman and the detective, who tried desperately to prevent his dropping the bomb which wrought such frightful havoc. In the flurry of the occasion, Harvey had not recovered his field glass from his friend, an oversight which he regretted, for it would have helped greatly in learning precisely what the Professor was doing. But his unaided eyes told him enough to suggest a shrewd guess.

"He is going to launch a bomb, and if he does, it won't be a giant cracker, which gave those young men such a big scare the other day."

A minute later came the tremendous report, and Harvey felt the ground tremble. A mass of smoke and flying fragments rose over the spot where the shanty had stood.

"He has blown up the building and every one in it!" gasped the startled youth. "I wonder whether the child has been hurt; Pendar can take care of himself."

Harvey hesitated whether to run to the spot, and had made up his mind to do so, when he was checked by an incident that in its way was as startling as the explosion.

It will be remembered that he had brought his aeroplane to rest in the large clearing in front of the humble home of Uncle Tommy Waters, the weather prophet. Had the circumstances been different, he would have given attention to the house and its occupants, but the thrilling incidents in course of happening elsewhere kept his eyes turned in the opposite direction, and the cabin might as well have been a hundred miles distant for all he knew of it for the time.

That which caught his attention with the suddenness of a snap of a whip in his ear and caused him to whirl the other way was a childish voice:

"Oh, isn't that a funny thing?"

Harvey Hamilton was struck speechless for a moment by the sight that greeted his eyes. Two little girls, one freckled, homely, and poorly dressed, the other pretty, with clustering curls and in fine clothes, stood side by side, no more than a dozen paces distant, staring wonderingly at him and the aeroplane. The third member of the group was an immense shaggy dog as black as midnight, which stood wagging his tail as if pleased with what he saw. In the door of the cabin behind them was the pudgy wife of Uncle Tommy, also staring and seemingly at a loss to comprehend the strange doings and sights. Uncle Tommy was not visible, having gone to Chesterton earlier in the day, with the time of his return uncertain.

Harvey beckoned the children to draw near. With some timidity they did so, the dog following as if to see that no harm befell either. The two halted a few steps away and smiled, the homely one with her forefinger between her lips and her head to one side. Her companion showed no embarrassment.

"Your name is Grace Hastings, isn't it?" asked the young aviator, in a kindly voice and with a rapidly beating heart.

"Yes,—what's your name?" she asked with winsome confidence.

"Harvey Hamilton; wouldn't you like to go home to mamma?"

"Oh, yes indeed; won't you——"

She suddenly broke down and sobbed.

"There, my dear; you mustn't cry, for we are going to take you home just as soon as we can; your papa and mamma want to see you badly and they shall not be kept waiting; won't you come closer?"

"May Peggy come too?" she asked with a smile, though the tears still wetted her plump cheeks.

"Certainly, for I know Peggy is a good girl."

"Yes, she is, and we love each other, don't we, Peggy?"

Grace looked at her companion for reply, and she nodded her head six or seven times but did not speak. The two advanced and Harvey took each by the hand.

"How long have you and Peggy known each other?" asked Harvey of Grace.

"This is the first time the bad folks would let me go to see her," was the reply.

The youth read the full meaning of these words. The kidnappers had kept the little one a close prisoner from the first. For the sake of her health, they probably allowed her to play at times near the shanty, as she was doing when he first saw her, but as the time of her captivity, as they viewed it, was shortened to a few hours, they yielded to her wish to walk the little way through the woods to her neighbor. She would be within quick reach, and besides, had promised to come back after a brief absence. What she might reveal while playing with Peggy Waters could not bring any risk of her loss to her captors. These facts, which became known afterward, showed that the flight of Harvey Hamilton's aeroplane on its first sweep over the ramshackle structure had not roused any distrust on the part of the two abductors there, who kept out of sight while the biplane was near.

The young man was stirred by the sight of the child standing before him, and chattering in her innocent way. Despite what had just occurred and the certainty that Professor Morgan had played havoc with the miscreants, the youth was uneasy. Some of the gang might have escaped and started upon other mischief. Grace was too much exposed to their evil intentions.

"Let us go into the house," said Harvey, taking each child by the hand and walking toward the dumpy woman who still filled the door of the cabin, staring as if she failed to understand what had taken place.

"Good morning," saluted Harvey; "if you don't mind we will go inside and sit down for a little while."

"I'm sure you're welcome," replied the housewife, stepping back to give room. "It seems to me there's been queer goings on around here. What made that awful noise I heerd a little while ago?"

"A friend of mine blew up the shanty where several villains were holding this little girl a prisoner."

"La sakes! You don't say so; did you ever hear of sich carryings on?"

She stood with her arms akimbo and stared at her caller, who had seated himself near the open door, where he could see his aeroplane and whatever might appear in the clearing. Grace and Peggy sat farther back, whispering and chuckling together, as new acquaintances do who have no idea of the fearful meaning of what is going on around them.

"Where is Uncle Tommy?" asked Harvey of the wife.

"He went to town two hours ago. You know," she added with natural pride, "that all the folks depends on him to know what kind of weather we're going to have, and he's gone to Chesterton to tell 'em."

"I have heard of his reputation as a weather prophet."

At this juncture, Grace rose abruptly from her chair and asked Harvey:

"How long have I been here?"

"Not knowing when you came I can't tell exactly, Grace, but I am sure it is only a short time."

"I promised Alessandro I wouldn't stay long and I must be going."

"Wait a little while; he won't care—."

"There he comes for me now! He will be angry and beat me," she exclaimed, standing beside her young friend and looking out of the door in a tremor of alarm.

Sure enough, the miscreant had come into plain sight. He was walking with bowed head and his hands behind him, as if the wrists were fastened together, and only one or two paces to the rear strode Detective Simmons Pendar, with a revolver ready for instant use. The picture told its own story.

"Stay where you are," said Harvey, laying a gentle hand on the shoulder of Grace Hastings; "Alessandro sha'n't hurt you."

With this assurance, the youth went down the few steps and advanced to meet his friend.

"I don't admire his looks," he remarked with a smile as he glanced at the swarthy, scowling face.

"He's as ugly as he looks," replied the detective.

"Is he the only one?"

"Professor Morgan's bomb sent one flying among the trees, where he will stay until carried away. And that is Grace Hastings?" said the officer, with a radiant face, as he looked at the winsome countenance in the doorway.

"She told me that that is her name, and I think she ought to know; but what do you mean to do with this fellow?"

"I have been thinking. You know there were three of them; I exchanged shots with Catozzi when we were starting with your aeroplane. I am anxious to capture him, but he was left at Chesterton, where he will probably wait till he receives more news."

"You can march this one ahead of you to the town and have him locked up."

The face of the detective became grave. He shook his head.

"I am afraid that if I do that, and the truth becomes known, as it surely will be, the people will lynch him."

"Who cares if they do?" asked Harvey; "it will serve him right."

"He and the others deserve it, but the law should deal with them. I have a better plan."

CHAPTER XXXI.
LYNCH LAW.

During this brief conversation between Harvey Hamilton and Detective Pendar, the prisoner stood slightly to one side with his bare head bent and his face looking like that of some baffled imp of darkness. Not only had he lost his pistol and stiletto, but his hands were useless to him. The weapons seemed not to have been on his person at the moment of the explosion, for his captor had seen nothing of them. Pendar looked at the woman.

"Have you a clothesline?"

"Of course I have, and I need it too," was the reply.

"Let me have it and I'll pay you enough to buy three new ones."

"That sounds sensible; what do you want to do with it?" asked Mrs. Waters, pleased with the chance of driving a good bargain.

"I wish to bind this scamp so fast that he will never be able to free himself."

"'Cording to what you tell me you oughter put it round his neck; I'll give you all the help I can; yes, you can have the rope," and she walked into the kitchen to bring the article, which, although knotted in several places, must have been fifty feet long.

"In there!" commanded the detective, motioning to Pierotti, who slouched through the door, the frightened little girl backing away and staring at him. Sullen, revengeful, but helpless, the Latin submitted to every indignity unresistingly. Pendar was an adept at such work and wound the rope in and out and around, again and again until every foot of it had been utilized, and the prisoner was bound so effectually that had he been one of the famous Davenport brothers he would have been unable to loosen his bonds.

"Now, Mrs. Waters," said the officer when he had completed his work, "you needn't have any fear of him."

"Fear of him!" repeated the woman with a sniff; "do you think the like of him could scare me? Do you see that poker?" she asked, pointing to the iron rod with the curved end leaning against the wall of the fireplace; "if he dares so much as open his mouth to speak to me, I'll break it over his head."

"A sensible idea!" exclaimed Harvey Hamilton; "don't forget it, and I hope he will give you an excuse for doing what you have in mind."

Man and youth stepped outside, where the latter waited for his friend to make clear his intentions.

"The thing I am most anxious to do," said the detective, "is to reach the nearest telegraph office as quickly as I can, that I may send a message to Horace Hastings and his wife with the news that will raise them from the depths of despair to perfect happiness."

"It will take us only a few minutes to reach Chesterton with the aeroplane."

"True, and we can carry the little girl with us. Besides, I sha'n't be satisfied until I have the nippers on the one still at large. Let us be off, for you have no idea how eager I am to send the tidings to the parents of Grace."

When the little one learned that she was about to be taken home to see her papa and mamma, she clapped her hands and danced with joy. She kissed Peggy good-bye, made the child promise to come and see her in her home in the distant city and then told Mr. Pendar she was ready.

Naturally she was timid when informed that she was to take a ride with the big bird, and she clung to her protector, who carefully adjusted himself with her in his lap. She promised not to stir or even speak while on the way. Harvey had headed his machine toward the longest stretch of open ground, and set the propeller revolving. Then he dashed forward, sprang into place and grasped the levers. The biplane was already moving at a rapidly accelerated pace over the withered grass, and at the proper point rose clear and sailed away to the eastward. The tiny passenger stared and tried to hold her breath when she realized that she was far above the treetops, but she gave not the slightest trouble to her friends.

The distance to Chesterton was so brief that it seemed our friends had hardly left the earth when they began coming down again. An easy landing was made in the open space in front of the hotel and Pendar lifted Grace out.

"Now you will go with me," he said, grasping her hand and hurrying down the main street to the telegraph office, which was several blocks from the hotel. "Harvey, you will look after your machine and I shall soon rejoin you."

It would be hard to describe the blissful joy with which the detective seized one of the yellow telegraph blanks and wrote these words, addressed to Horace Hastings:

"I have Grace with me, perfectly well and unharmed. She asks me to give her love to papa and mamma and to say that she is coming home just as quickly as she can. As I shall be needed here for some time yet, perhaps you would better come for her. One of the kidnappers is dead, one a prisoner, and I hope soon to have the third."

"PENDAR."

Brief as was the absence of the detective from the hotel, the interval had been sufficient for a terrifying situation to develop. A larger crowd than usual gathered at sight of the little girl sitting on the lap of the man supposed to be a commercial traveler, and when the two hurried down the street, there were eager inquiries as to what it meant. An instinctive feeling of caution led Harvey to make evasive answers, for he feared to tell the truth to the excited crowd; but he could not falsify and was pressed so hard that he was literally forced to give the facts. The little girl, who had walked down the street with the supposed commercial traveler, was Grace Hastings, kidnapped some time before in Philadelphia, and the man who had her in charge was one of the most famous detectives in the country.

The story sounded so incredible that for a minute or two it was not believed. Every member of the group had read of the unspeakable crime, and their feelings were stirred to the depths. Parents especially were insistent that no punishment was too severe for the authors of the cruel wrong.

"And one of them was that fellow who fired his pistol at the detective when he was starting off with you in your flying machine?" demanded a red-faced listener.

Harvey nodded.

"He was; where is he now?"

"Yes; where is he?"

A dozen glanced in different directions. Could they have laid hands on the miscreant his life would not have been worth a moment's purchase.

"I saw him hurrying down the street, right after the flying machine left," explained a large boy on the edge of the crowd.

"Where was he going?" demanded the first speaker.

"I didn't ask him and I don't 'spose he'd told if I had."

"But you've got one of 'em?" said another man to Harvey.

"Yes; one was killed by the explosion, but the other wasn't hurt to any extent."

"Where is he?"

"Safely bound in the house of Uncle Tommy Waters."

Uncle Tommy was in the group, somewhat back, chewing hard and listening to the absorbing relation. He had not yet spoken, but did not allow a word to escape him. The instant the last remark was made, he stopped chewing, pushed nearer the young aviator and asked:

"Did you say he's in my house?"

"Yes, bound fast in a chair and under the watchful eye of your wife."

"Do you mean to tell me that consarned critter is a-settin' in my parlor this minute and talking love to Betsey?" roared the wrathful Uncle Tommy, in a still higher voice.

"I don't think he is trying to make love to your wife; if he does, she has the poker at hand and she told me she would use it if he gave her the least excuse."

The weather prophet boiled over. Ignoring the youth who had given the infuriating news, he addressed the crowd:

"Do you hear that, folks? That limb of Satan is a-settin' in my front parlor and Betsey hasn't any one with her! It's the most outrageous outrage that was ever outraged. Do you 'spose I'm goin' to stand it?"

"What will you do about it?" asked a neighbor tauntingly.

"What will I do 'bout it? I'll show him. He's one of the varmints that stole that sweet innercent child. Let's lynch him!"

The proposal struck fire on the instant. Nothing is so excitable as an American crowd, and an impetuous leader can do anything with it. A dozen voices shouted:

"That's it! lynch him! lynch him! come on, boys! we're together in this."

The last words were uttered by a tall, middle-aged farmer without coat or vest. He had a clear, ringing voice, as if born to command. In a twinkling he was at the head of the swarm which was increasing in numbers every minute, with every one ardent to carry out the startling proposal first made by Uncle Tommy Waters.

Harvey Hamilton was alarmed. It has been shown that he had not a shadow of sympathy for the criminal, who was bound in the cabin of the weather prophet, but he knew the detective's sentiments. He had left the prisoner behind in order to save him from the very fate that now threatened, and which had been precipitated by the truth the youth saw no way of holding back from them.

Standing beside his silent machine, Harvey shouted:

"You mustn't do that! It is contrary to law; the courts will punish him; leave him to them!"

"Yes," sneered the leader, halting long enough to exchange a few words; "he won't be in jail more than three months when he'll be pardoned or they'll let him out on parole; it'll cost money to convict him and we'll save the State the expense."

"You are mistaken; there is too much resentment over this Black Hand business to show any mercy to the criminals."

"That's what's the matter with this crowd; come on, boys!"

The mob was moving off, when Detective Pendar, still holding the hand of Grace Hastings, came hurrying from the street to the front of the hotel. He read the meaning of what he heard and saw, and raised his hand for attention.

"I appreciate your feelings, my friends, but you mustn't stain the fair name of Pennsylvania by such an illegal deed as you have in mind. The law will punish these men. Here is the little child, and you can see she has not been harmed in the least."

It was an unfortunate appeal. The sight of the frightened girl and the knowledge that she was the victim of a most cruel wrong, roused the fury of the men to a white heat. The protesting detective was swept aside like chaff, and the whole party broke into a run for the home of Uncle Tommy Waters, with the weather prophet himself in the lead.

CHAPTER XXXII.
MYSTERIES ARE EXPLAINED.

If the wrathful Uncle Tommy Waters could have looked in upon his home at the time Harvey Hamilton was telling his story, he would have seen there was no ground for misgiving so far as the partner of his joys was concerned.

A muscular woman, with a big iron poker in hand, a massive dog nosing about the house and ready at instant call, surely had little to fear from a man whose wrists were encircled by steel bracelets and who was swathed like a mummy in a network of rope, no matter how sinister his mood might be. She, too, had heard from her husband the story of the kidnapping of little Grace Hastings, and having a child of her own of about the same age, she gave it as her honest opinion that every one of the criminals should be burned at the stake, thrown head first into a well, tumbled over the highest precipice in the world, and then left to perish with cold in the region discovered by Commander Peary and not discovered by Dr. Cook.

When she found herself alone with the horrible villain, she told Peggy to go outside and play with the dog, while she had a little talk with the prisoner.

She seated herself a couple of paces in front of him, and looking piercingly into his glittering black eyes, demanded in a low, ominous voice:

"Now, what do you think of yourself? Don't speak a word or I'll bang you with this poker," and she raised the stiff rod threateningly.

Understanding what was said to him, the prisoner prudently held his peace.

"I asked you what you thought of yourself. What oughter be done with a scamp that steals a little child from its father and mother? Hanging is too good for him. Ain't you ashamed? Look out! Don't you dare open your mouth!"

And again the primitive weapon was brandished close to the captive's crown, whose shaggy wealth of hair could not have shielded it had the poker descended.

"You ask me what I think," finally blurted Pierotti in desperation; "you say you strike if I open mouth; I think you are mighty big fool,—that's what I think—now you know."

As the Italian sat he faced the open door, toward which the back of the woman was turned. While striving to grasp the meaning of the broken sentences, she saw from the expression of the impish countenance that he was looking at some one behind her. She whirled about, and almost fell from her chair, for standing in the doorway was a second member of the Black Hand, in the person of Amasi Catozzi, who had been slightly wounded by the revolver of Detective Pendar.

This criminal, quick to read the meaning of the departure of the officer with the young aviator, in an outburst of uncontrollable passion fired at him, and then made all haste to the headquarters in the woods, whither his companion had preceded him. He was still running when the explosion told its horrifying story. He knew what had taken place as well as if he had been an eyewitness, with the exception of the personal results to his two associates. With a raging chagrin which no one can comprehend, he saw that the princely ransom which he had felt in the itching palm of his hand had slipped away forever. All that remained to him was to save his own neck, as well as that of the survivors, if so be there were any, provided he could bring about such a consummation without adding to his own peril.

Skilfully keeping out of sight in the wood, he saw Alessandro Pierotti handcuffed and driven to the cabin as a prisoner. Catozzi would have felt a gleeful delight in shooting the man with whom he had already exchanged shots, but to do that would have intensified his own danger, since it would have added ardor to the efforts to run him to earth. The certain result of such disaster would be a verdict of murder, when kidnapping at most involved only a sentence to a long term of imprisonment, with the cheering prospect of a speedy pardon in the background, or a release upon parole, and the opportunity to resume his atrocious misdeeds. Consequently, Catozzi did not interfere during the first part of the proceedings.

As stealthily as a red Indian he peered out from the depth of the forest. Waiting until the detective and child accompanied the young aviator in his flight to Chesterton and were gone long enough for him to feel no fear of their return, he went forward and presented himself in the door while the pointed and somewhat one-sided conversation was going on between Mrs. Waters and the bound prisoner in the chair.

It would have pleased the new arrival to give the woman her final quietus, but he was restrained by the same knowledge that stayed his hand when he might have shot Simmons Pendar. She was so terrified that she could only stare in a daze at Catozzi, with a limp grasp upon the simple weapon in her hand. She would have begged for mercy had she not quickly seen that it was not necessary. The Italian merely glanced at her, and striding forward to the chair, speedily cut the thongs and the prisoner rose to his feet. The loosening of the handcuffs would require more time and could wait. The two talked briefly in their own language. Pierotti indulged in the luxury of a hideous grimace at the woman as he was following his companion out of the door and across the clearing to the forest, into which they plunged and were immediately lost to sight.

This explanation will make clear the disappointment of the mob which swarmed out of the wood soon afterward, with the panting Uncle Tommy still at the head, and the worried detective beside him. He had turned over the care of Grace Hastings to Harvey Hamilton, who remained behind at Chesterton. In his flurry and eagerness Uncle Tommy caught the toe of his boot at the threshold and sprawled on his hands and knees into the "parlor" of his residence.

"Is my lamb safe?" he asked, scrambling to his feet and gazing at the pudgy figure still seated and maintaining a somewhat stronger grip upon the poker.

"You old simpleton! Why don't you clean your boots?" was the loving response of his life partner, who quickly regained her natural disposition when she saw that all danger had gone by.

Her story was quickly told. The disappointment to all, except the detective, was keen, and his feelings were solely due to his respect for law and order. Uncle Tommy was asked whether his dog could not take the scent of the two fugitives and run them down, but the weather prophet replied that the canine wasn't worth a shoestring for such work.

"You never will be able to find the couple in the woods," said Pendar; "there are too many hiding places; they can dodge you for weeks; the only course is for us to return to Chesterton at once, and for me to telegraph to all the surrounding towns, asking the authorities to be on the lookout for them. They will have to leave the woods sooner or later and there is a fair chance of catching both."

He added in a lower voice:

"What is left of one of them lies a little way from here; the body must not be neglected."

The announcement caused a striking change in the moods of all. Three of the men walked forth with the detective and viewed all that remained of the Black Hander. One of them carried a blanket which was tenderly laid over the body.

"It is best not to remove it until the coroner has given permission," explained the officer; "since there has been a death he must make an investigation."

The party straggled back to town, Uncle Tommy being the only one who stayed behind. Detective Pendar having decided upon his course acted promptly. When he entered the telegraph office he found a long message from Mr. Hastings awaiting him. It was so fervent in its expressions of gratitude that the eyes of the detective filled and he could not command his voice for some minutes. The telegram contained a loving message to the child, and the assurance that the father would start for Chesterton at once to bring her home.

Pendar sent notices to all the nearby towns and to the large cities, doing his work so thoroughly that he said to himself as he lighted a cigar and leaned back in his chair:

"If those two fellows can break through the net that I have spread round them, they will almost deserve to get away. They may keep in hiding for several days, but sooner or later they will be gathered in."

Harvey Hamilton proposed to carry Grace in his aeroplane to Philadelphia, confident that by starting early the next morning he could reach her home by noon, but his friend showed him the folly of anything of that nature. She was unaccustomed to riding in the air, and an accident was more than likely. Moreover, her father was due in Chesterton on the afternoon of the morrow.

"The child has already passed through too much to incur any more danger from which it is possible to save her. And that reminds me, Harvey," added the detective with a smile, "you have decided by this time who it was that chopped up your aeroplane."

"It must have been Catozzi and Caprioni."

"Beyond a doubt."

"Why did they do it?"

"They may have seen a possible danger in the presence of a machine like that in the neighborhood of Chesterton and decided to put it out of commission."

"Why didn't they do the same with my second?"

"It would have involved a great deal more risk, and could have accomplished little or nothing for them. Besides, we mustn't forget the element of unadulterated cussedness that actuates so many members of mankind. Professor Morgan took a fancy to inspect your machine at close range without the chance of meeting you, and so he made a visit early in the morning, only to find it smashed to everlasting smithereens. He left, your colored boy being just in time to gain a glimpse of him, and straightway telegraphed your father, and you know what followed."

This part of my story may be summed up in a few sentences. On the morrow the coroner entered into an official investigation, as in duty bound, of the death of the Italian supposed to be Giuseppe Caprioni, blown up by the explosion of a bomb. The testimony of Professor Milo Morgan was much needed, but he had departed no one knew whither, and that of Simmons Pendar supplied its place. The verdict was in accordance with the facts, so far as they could be ascertained, and the body was buried in Potter's Field.

The next day the gratifying intelligence came that both Catozzi and Pierotti had been captured in Groveton, only twelve miles from Chesterton. Driven out by hunger they had applied at a house for food, and were quickly arrested. They were tried, found guilty and sentenced to the longest terms possible in State Prison, where it is to be hoped they will spend the remainder of their days.

Horace Hastings reached Chesterton by special train earlier than was expected and took his child home with him.

CHAPTER XXXIII.
WHERE IS BOHUNKUS?

Harvey Hamilton stayed in Chesterton till the close of the incidents just narrated. His interest was so stirred that he had no wish to leave before their conclusion. During the hours of waiting, he made several short flights in his aeroplane, and when he and Detective Pendar were called upon to give their evidence the flying machine was convenient. In addition, he gave several of the townsmen the most thrilling experiences of their lives. He invited Uncle Tommy Waters to accompany him on an aerial excursion, but a million dollars would not have tempted the old gentleman to take his feet off the firm earth.

A seemingly small matter gave the young aviator anxiety. Upon his return from the explosion of the shanty, he expected to find Bohunkus Johnson either sitting on the porch of the hotel or strolling about the town. Although the colored youth was offended by the brusque reproof of Harvey, it was not his nature to hold a grudge, and his friend was prepared to meet him half way and apologize for his hasty words, but no Bohunkus showed up. The night passed without his appearance. Harvey went to his room in the early morning only to find that his bed had not been occupied.

"He has gone home," was the conclusion of the youth. "If he wishes to pout I shall not interfere, but he ought to have left some word for me."

While waiting in Chesterton, Harvey wrote a letter to his father, giving a full account of the recovery of little Grace Hastings, her restoration to her parents and the capture of the two surviving members of the Black Hand, which, as has been stated, was duly followed by their sentence to long terms in the penitentiary. This letter was crossed by one from his father, which confirmed the explanation made by Mr. Pendar of the wrecking of the first aeroplane. He had received quick notice of the misfortune from Professor Morgan, and sympathizing with his son had provided him with a second flying machine in record time. When a young man who took an aerial ride with Harvey told him he had seen the two supposed commercial travelers in the vicinity of the hotel sheds at daylight of the eventful morning, the last shadow of doubt was removed as to the identity of the offenders.

Mr. Hastings paid over the entire reward to Simmons Pendar, who would have insisted that one-half of the large sum should go to Harvey Hamilton, had the latter not notified him that any such proposition would be accepted as an insult.

Despite a feeling of vexation, Harvey became so concerned over Bohunkus that he finally telegraphed to Mr. Cecil Hartley, the farmer to whom the colored boy had been bound years before, and asked whether he was at home. The reply was that he had not been seen since he left in the aeroplane with Harvey. This was disquieting news and the youth did not know what to make of it. Had not Detective Pendar been absent just then he would have applied to him for counsel. Enlightenment, however, came from an unexpected quarter.

It was on the evening of the second day, after the guests at the hotel had eaten supper and left the dining-room, that the landlord came out and sat down near Harvey, who occupied a chair at the farther end of the porch. The boniface was chuckling as if in good humor over something. Harvey wondered what it could be.

"You ain't worrying about that darkey of yours?" was the first question.

"I am not worried so much as I am curious," replied the youth; "he took offense the other day because I reproved him for an act of stupidity, but it is not his nature to sulk so long. I thought he had gone home, but learned a short while ago that he hasn't been there."

"Oh, no; he's a long way from home by this time."

"Do you know where he is?" asked the startled Harvey.

"Not precisely, but I reckon I can make a good guess."

"Please do so."

"You remember that after that queer crank that they call Professor Morgan had blowed up the headquarters of them kidnappers, he did not stay in them parts."

"No; I noticed he headed for Chesterton."

"That's where he came; he landed in the shed yard near the spot where your machine was smashed and had hardly touched the airth when that darkey of yours was there and the two begun talking together mighty earnest."

"Do you know what it was about?" asked Harvey, in whose mind a sudden suspicion had formed.

"I don't know what was said at first, 'cause they was too fur off for me to hear, but they hadn't been talking more'n five minutes—maybe not that long—when they walked up on the porch and sot down. I was standing a few feet from them looking out at the things which was beginning to hum, so I heard about all that was said. What do you 'spose it was about?"

"I can make a guess, but I prefer you should tell me."

"That darkey said something about his father that was a famous chief in Africa that he'd like to visit, and he asked the Professor if he couldn't take him there. The Professor said nothing in the world was easier, though he wasn't sure his machine was quite ready, but it would be very soon. He had made a lot of wonderful inventions and had figured out things so he could keep afloat in the air for nigh twenty-four hours. They would have to do better than that to cross the Atlantic Ocean, but he hadn't any doubt he would soon have matters settled so there would be no trouble. As near as I could make out, the Professor invited him to go along and stay with him while he finished some experiments and got things fixed so he could remain aloft for two or three weeks, without taking aboard any new ile."

"And Bohunkus agreed to that!" exclaimed Harvey.

"If that is the darkey's name, he jumped at the chance. The Professor's idea was to wait at the hotel here for two or three days, till matters sort of quieted down, but the African insisted they should start at once."

"That perhaps was natural, but did he give any reasons for his haste?"

The landlord chuckled again.

"He said it was on your account; you was always interfering with his affairs, and you'd be sure to make objections; you meant well, but you didn't know much and they would have trouble with you if they didn't leave before you got back. I hope you ain't offended with the words I'm telling you."

"Offended!" repeated Harvey, "that good-hearted fellow couldn't offend me; I only feel concern because he has placed himself in the hands of a lunatic."

"That's the Professor and no mistake. Well, the darkey had it all his own way. Not long after, they walked out to the shed yards and shot away in that outlandish machine that doesn't make any noise and travels like a greased streak of lightning. Before they started, the Professor told the darkey he must not write any letter of explanation to you."

"Did he do so?"

"He didn't think of it at first, but the Professor had reminded him, so he went to his own room and wrote without his knowledge."

"What did he do with the letter?"

"Gave it to me."

"And why didn't you hand it to me?" asked Harvey.

"'Cause I had to promise I wouldn't till this evening after supper. The darkey explained that if you got it too soon, you'd butt in and upset things and he didn't mean to have anything like that. Here's the letter."

And the landlord drew a missive from his inner coat pocket and handed it to Harvey, remarking as he did so:

"I had a mind to give it to you as soon as you and the detective got back, for I didn't feel right about that outlandish scheme of the Professor, but I had made my promise and stuck to it."

Excusing himself, Harvey Hamilton walked into the writing-room, and under the glare of the gaslight unfolded a sheet of paper which was not inclosed in an envelope. He recognized the scrawling hand that had written his name on the outside and read the following amazing communication. The only liberty I have taken with it is in the way of punctuation, in order to help make clear the meaning:

"DEER HARV:

"doan' think ime mad at U, coz I aint,—its all right; I think a bully lot of U. Me and the purfesser start 2 day for Afriky to make a vizzit to my dad, the grate cheef Foozleum, when i cum back, ile bring U a nelefunt that we'll hang in a nett under the masheen. I meen to fetch a graff 2 [several other spellings of this difficult word were crossed out], as we can cut a hole in the top of the dragging of the Skize and let his head stick thru; doan' try to foller us, 'cause U can't carry nuff ighl to keep the steem agoing no more,—with luv.

BUNK."

Harvey smiled at this phonetic system run mad. Then an expression of worriment clouded his countenance.

"Poor Bunk! You don't know what you are doing. You have gone into a danger from which heaven alone can save you; but I shall do all I can without wasting an hour, though I fear it is too late."

And what Harvey Hamilton did and all that befell Bohunkus Johnson in his aerial flight with Professor Morgan will be told in "THE FLYING BOYS TO THE RESCUE."